Seductive
Vibrations

B.J. Priestley

Seductive Vibrations

DEDICATION

Dedicated to all my followers on Facebook, Twitter and Instagram. Without your support, I would not have got to where I am now. The amazing responses already from the book is merely wonderful, watching how my scripts have facilitated so many women, in so many different ways.

CONTENTS

Seductive Vibrations

ACKNOWLEDGMENTS

Thank you to all the beta readers who helped make this possible.

Seductive Vibrations

WHAT AM I DOING?

Jolting upright in bed, looking around I begin to wonder how I'd gotten here, Of course, I know how I came to be here, I just don't see how my entire life has shifted so drastically in only a few short months. I've been having this dream, or rather nightmare a lot lately, and it proceeds to constantly wake me up. Hoping it wasn't true, I'd normally push it to the rear of my head, attempting to forget it, straining to cover it. The crazy thing is, I am not this type of person at all, He has taken over my life, changed me so much, I don't recognise myself anymore, that is a lie, I see my old self, the old me I lost years ago. I wish to recognise where things are going next, but right now I feel like I'm losing control of my life, I was happily ensconced in my little routine. I'd go to university, then to work, then I'd go home; simple, and uncomplicated. He's turned everything upside down, I can't find my way back and even if I could, I don't think I'd want to. He makes me happy, sitting here on his bed, still somewhat shaken up, I can't conceive of anything else but the same recurring nightmare, is he making me happy enough, or is this simply one big mistake? Hearing the door unfastened, I know instantly it is him without even looking, when he walks into a room, I pick up on it straight away, putting up my head I look towards the door and sure enough, there he is.

"Good morning baby, you look refreshed" I can't help but grin at him, somehow he has defined all odds, made me want to live life again, and love it.

"I guess I have you to thank for that" I say sheepishly, my cheeks flushing pink, even after he's seen me at my most vulnerable, I still feel insecure. I can't help but avert my eyes whenever he calls me baby.

"I thought that maybe today we could have some fun?" His body climbing onto the bed, I begin to laugh.

"No, I don't mean that kind of fun, unless that's what you require? I mean we could just stay in all day and explore each other more..." His body moving closer to me, how is he always in such a good mood? His hands started grabbing my body, I can't help but laugh, I jump back, my hand throwing up telling him to stop.

"No Jackson, I think we can behave for today, I have

things that I need to do anyway. I have to go to my apartment as I haven't been back there all week" He pouted looking down at me, my breathing quickening under his gaze.

"Plus, I promised Daz I'd meet up with him and his girlfriend" I've got to admit, I have missed my apartment so much, and it seems like forever since I last saw my friends. We've spent two weeks in his room, hardly leaving. I skipped university, I am guessing I have lost my job as well now.

"Fine, come on babes, let's get you home" Getting ready, we walked to the car, climbing in he started the engine.

"Hey, can you take me to the centre, I need to grab a few things, I will make my way home from there" Smiling at him, I slightly nudge his arm, as he begins to drive.

"Of course, babes" We sit quietly, after 15 minutes, finally reaching the centre he parks up the shops surrounding us, kissing him I climb out the car.

"Catch you after baby" He smiles, driving off down the street, turning I begin to walk into the shops, shopping was dull, as always, I hate shopping, I detest a lot of girly stuff, just give me a blanket and a chick flick and I am happy. Getting home the flat is quiet, too quiet in fact. It feels so surreal, I haven't been alone for two weeks. Things have changed so much, there is no going back now, there is no way I can go back to being the person I used to be. Appearing about the flat I can't help but smile seeing the kitchen, the kitchen that changed so much in one night, even so I still possess a sense of doom the feeling never leaving no matter what I do.

1 BIRTHDAY PARTY

The sound of the alarm waking me, I hate work, I hate university and I hate mornings. Hitting the button, I look around, my life is nothing amazing, I live with my roommates, I spend most of my time here, university or work. I should be waking up in a hotel room somewhere, but no, I failed at that this year. Groggily walking to the shower, I climb in, the water feeling amazing, today needs to go fast, tonight, even faster I honestly need tomorrow to arrive like now. Climbing out, getting dried my eyes looking around I will be home soon, tonight won't be long or late, then I can just relax here. Walking out my bedroom it is quiet, grabbing food, I embark on walking to university, I don't like driving if it isn't too far, my mind is flying away every thought running through it. Walking in I can't help but smile, a few hours to take my mind off today, yet deep down I know that isn't going to happen, not at all.

"Hi Alena" Looking up it is Megan, a friend at university, I wouldn't consider her a friend just someone I see a lot here, once I leave I don't hear from her or keep in touch.

"Hi Megan, how are you" Smiling at her, I sit down, she takes the seat next to me.

"Good, going away tonight for a week, I can't wait, it's my sister's wedding in 5 days so looking forward to it" She looks so happy, smiling I just nod, I am not a people person, I just want to get my course done and leave, to be honest that sounds crazy and mean but I like a simple life now. Sitting the class took ages, my mind trying to concentrate, but I just can't, looking at the clock, today is going slow, maybe I should have just stayed in bed all day and slept? Getting to 12pm, walking out of the university I walk to the bakers, grabbing food I start on the journey to the office, getting in I sit down, keeping my head down I begin working, watching the clock. Every minute feels like an hour, why is today going so slow? I need to stay at work late tonight, it's my birthday and I would rather avoid it at all costs, I have not celebrated my birthday in so many years. The issue is I work in Telesales, there are no goals to meet to go home, so as soon as it reaches six o'clock I have to leave, no overtime nothing. Sitting here watching the time tick by, you can tell I am not working. My voice sounds fed up, lazy and like I don't want to be here, I do want to be here, but I know I can't stay here till tomorrow, I can't use it as an excuse to escape my birthday, when it reaches six, everyone else starts packing up and finishing, rushing to get home, me I go at snail pace, as slow as I can just to avoid tonight. Grabbing my items, I start to make my way out, walking home, I just know I can't escape tonight at all. Maybe it won't be as bad as I think? Granted, I have not celebrated a birthday since I first got with Max, birthdays are not something to celebrate, that is when all the abuse started, on my birthday. I am hoping it is something at the flat, a small party, nothing too big. Opening the door, I begin bracing myself for a flat full of people I do not know, here to celebrate my birthday, turning the light on the flat is empty, not even Georgina or Liam is in. Well, this is a benefit, smiling I begin walking in I head straight to the fridge to grab a drink, noticing the note on it.

"GET READY, GET DRESSED AND GET BEAUTIFUL I WILL BE BACK AT 7!

-   GEORGINA"

Ever the urgent, can't just write in lower case can she, the thing is I avoid my birthday every year, I plan trips away, go to my parents anything to avoid Georgina's mad, crazy parties. This year I was so busy with university and work I forgot about my birthday coming up, I forgot to plan something and when Georgina brought it up, it was already too late, she had planned my birthday party, clearly it was not here though. Well, I guess I should get ready, the last thing I want is Georgina coming back, me not ready and get her complaining that we will be late. Jumping in the shower just standing here wondering what is happening tonight, I have a bad feeling about it though, but I should enjoy myself, I should for a change celebrate that I am alive. Getting dried, I start looking through the cupboard, what can I wear? Thinking of Georgina, my eyes glance at the dresses, something that never gets worn, to be honest though I don't want to wear a dress. It is my birthday, I want to feel comfortable and not like I am going over the top, so I will just grab some Jeans and a shirt, add a black pair of boots and it is a safe bet, comfy yet suitable for pubs, clubs, cinema everything pretty much. Walking in the living room, I have half an hour before seven, so I guess I will spend half an hour tonight like I want, sitting on the sofa, I grab the remote, turning it on I put my feet up, watching the tv. Glancing up at the clock it is five past seven, Georgina is late as always. A few minutes into the next program the door unlocks, Georgina stood there looking at me shocked.

"You're not ready yet? I left a note saying to be ready for seven, did you not see it?" She runs over her hands grabbing mine, pulling me from the sofa.

"I am ready, see I don't wear these to work, do I?" Looking at her I can't help wondering what she thought I was going to wear.

"Not a chance, you're wearing something better than that" Her finger pointing at me up and down, she disapproves not a shock, I had a feeling this would happen. Looking at her in shock my head shaking, she just smiles.

"When was the last time you went out, like out, out and actually enjoyed yourself, and showed yourself off? Before Max so move it" Walking to me she begins dragging me in the bedroom, she threw open the closet doors, rifling through it as she does, she is throwing clothes over her shoulder, always messy as well, I can't help but smile. She turned around throwing a dress at me.

"Put this on and hurry up we are late!" Grabbing the dress, I look at it, yeah, this is Georgina's style not mine. Low cut, very low cut, black thigh high dress, with a slit, slipping into it, I feel like I have nothing on. Grabbing another pair of shoes, I put them on.

"Right I am ready" I stand there looking at her, feeling like I look amazing, her face fell, okay, she disapproves of the shoes I knew she would, flat simple and no heels.

"Put these on, don't wear them you're not fifty Alena, actually just throw them out altogether" Grabbing the shoes I start putting them on, standing up feeling myself wobbly from the heel height.

Standing in front of the mirror, I look at myself, I am nothing special, not even average, my hair bright red, hard to miss, green eyes slender yes, but still not good. Georgina's arm wrapped around me.

"We look amazing don't we" She grinned, turning to look at her reflection. Now Georgina is amazing, long legs, blue eyes, auburn hair, her body is amazing, the benefit of going to the gym, Georgina is the woman every man hangs around at clubs and bars hoping for a chance. Me stood here next to her, I have no chance with any guys, she is stunning, I am less than average.

"Come on we will be late, the taxi has been waiting for us" She again grabs my arm, pulling a little too quick and hard again, I wobble and nearly fall, I hate heels, I hate my birthday, and sometimes I hate Georgina for making me go out. Walking downstairs we climb into the taxi, my nerves kicking in, stomach flipping and worry rising inside me, I have not been out since just after I met Max, my ex, a person I want to forget, and move on from, a person who destroyed my life so quickly. Truth is, I have not been the same since Max, I can't, I seem to be stuck in the mind space of being afraid to leave my house, afraid of men, afraid of myself, but mostly I have no self-esteem left at all, none, every bit has been ripped away from me. While I kept trying to find it, every time I found a bit of self-esteem his face was there in my mind ready to steal it away.

"What? Oh yeah. We'll be there in two minutes, stop complaining" Georgina's voice snapping me out of my memories, she hung up the phone turning to face me smiling.

"Just Liam complaining we are late, you will love it, honestly Alena you will" Liam is our flat mate, he is into all things tech, gaming, cameras, computers, I don't see the fascination with it all to be honest, why waste time sat there pressing buttons? He is nice though, he has mousy-blond hair and green eyes, he is like a brother to me, training to be an electrician at university. The taxi stopped, looking up the big lights there, a night club, of all the places, Georgina picks a night club. My mind is screaming at me to run, and fast, just go home and avoid all this, but the effort Georgina has put into this, I can't be so cruel. Walking in the music is loud, that doesn't bother me, it is the mass of people I don't know that worries me.

"I invited everyone, so I hired it just for your party, so you will know everyone" Georgina smiles, hugging me, I look around there is no one here I know, where is Liam I know him I can't stop myself laughing at the thought she thinks I know these people. Walking in people keep coming over, you would expect them to be coming to wish me happy birthday, instead they just smile at me and greet Georgina, some not even noticing me. Walking through the crowds my eyes spot Liam, finally, I can see him, he is standing with someone, no doubt another student from the university.

"Look Liam is there, who is that with him?" Georgina walks ahead, reaching them, she stops and hugs the guy. He is big, his arms have tattoos on them, and while I am walking towards them, I feel like I am going super slow, staring at him, why do I feel such a pull towards this guy I don't even know? My heart is racing, I feel like there is a magnet drawing me to him, my hair standing up. Georgina's arm is rubbing against his, just like Georgina would do with a hot guy. Reaching them, he turns, and I am frozen, wow I can't stop myself staring, who is he?

"You must be Alena, Happy birthday" My eyes look up to him, he is big, muscle wise big, he has tattoos on his neck as well, his smile so soft and gentle, why do I feel an urge to touch him, why do his tattoos make me so weak?

"Hi" Really is that all I can think of saying? Hi and it is weak, I should be more like Georgina, confident and rubbing his arm making it known I am interested.

"Alena, this is Jackson, my brother" I look towards Liam, his brother? The difference is massive, Jackson stands is around 5ft 9" and his hair is amazing, why is my hair standing up, I feel like I just walked into a freezer.

"Oh, hey and thank you" Finally words exist in my mouth, I must look like a right fool, but something about him makes me want him, it is making me nervous, I have not felt this way in ages, I want to touch him, looking towards Georgina I see it on her face as well, in that case I have no chance, no chance at all if she is interested I don't stand a chance. So, I will give up the fight before it even starts, she wins, she gets him I will just wait for tonight to end.

"Well, let's get a drink first and tonight you are dancing Alena" Georgina drags me to the bar, Jackson watches as we walked off.

"Wow, who would have thought Liam's brother would be so hot? I mean, yeah, okay Liam isn't bad, but wow the difference" She smiled at me, I certainly have no chance, not even in hell would I have a chance.

"He is yes, good luck" I give in, just like that I won't win I won't fight for a guy either and clearly, I am not ready. Fact is, I don't get why women fight over a guy, I don't get why a guy can cheat and rather than being angry at the guy the women fight over him like he's a perfect man, I for one won't fight to win a guy. Grabbing our drinks, we walk back to Liam and Jackson sits down, I start drinking, I feel so out of place here, like I am in a place full of people who know each other, and I know no one, the plus side is there is booze, so I will stay for a few hours then go home, no doubt Georgina and Liam will be here all night.

"Come dance" Georgina grabs me, pulling me up, I so hate dancing, standing with her, I dance, feeling out of place and watching as guys crowd around us, I seriously hate this, I feel like I have no space to breath, the song finishes, I make a run for it, sitting back down at the table.   Liam and Jackson are standing near the dance floor, watching Liam walk onto it, beginning to dance, Georgina grabs Jackson pulling him on the dance floor, her body all over him, her hands grabbing him, and stroking his body I so feel sorry for him, yet at the same time I am laughing inside, I feel for any guy who agrees to dance with Georgina.   She is not subtle, if she likes you and your dancing with her, you will know and not be able to escape easily. Picking up my phone I look at the time, it is nearly twelve, time passes quickly when you want to go home apparently, but at least I can leave soon, I will give it an hour, I need to be at work tomorrow so can't stay too late, and I need my job too much to call in sick.   Watching Jackson makes a slip, escaping Georgina, she looks for him and quits, I wonder where he has gone? Georgina starts dancing with another guy, I admire her confidence, and ability to make it known she likes someone.

"Hey" Crap, jumping I turn and there he is standing behind me, he walks around and sits next to me, covered in sweat.

"I see Georgina is testing your dance skills" Laughing at him, he looks worn out.

"That is her testing dance skills? I would hate to see her trying it on with a guy" He laughs sitting back.

"She is feisty isn't she" His head shaking as he looks towards where she is dancing.

"Yes, that is Georgina for you, you didn't seem to be doing too bad with your dancing, let's be honest" He laughs looking at me like I have lost my mind.

"I was hoping I would fall over or pass out or anything to escape her, she really is not easy to slip away from is she" Laughing I have to agree, she isn't not at all.

"When she finds something, she likes she does not tend to let go or let it slip between her fingers, so you should be glad" He looked at me then towards where Georgina is dancing, shaking his head.

"Not my type, not at all, anyway enough of her, it is your birthday, Liam was saying you're studying business and accounting?" He is looking at me like he is interested in what I have to say, how is that even possible when he can easily have Georgina?

"Yes, I am. I want to eventually start my own business, what I don't know, but it would be good to have accounting as well, cut down costs and stuff you know" I smile at him, he is the first guy other than Liam I feel okay around, not like I need to run.

"That is good, I run my own businesses, a lot of work, but you know worth it in the end, something you can pass on to younger generations" I agree with that.

"Ah, right, I always thought you was in the navy or was Liam just trying to big up his brother before we met him?" I can't help but laugh it is something

15

Liam would do, and he did say Jackson was in the navy.

"No, I am in the navy, I am home now, though more than likely to stay, I don't think I will have any missions to do anymore" So he is in the navy then.

"That will explain why we have not met you in the two years we have known Liam then" We haven't, but then again, Liam has not met any of my family, I mean there is only my dad and step mum, but still he hasn't met them.

"Yeah, while he is my brother, we are close, but not that close, there is a lot he doesn't know about me and my life, which is how I like to keep it" I wonder why, then again, I know Liam, he can be a child at times, so I suspect certain aspects of Jacksons life, needs adults not children.

"So, why don't you think you will be going on any more missions?" Maybe that was too personal to ask? He looks like he is debating telling me.

"I have been doing it now over ten years, I could stop any time I want, and I feel now is the right time, but I always feel pulled back in. Honestly, I think it is time to say goodbye to that part of my life now" He seems so genuine, caring and kind, it amazes me how he is still sitting here with me rather than Georgina, looking down at myself, I certainly am not anything special. Sitting we talked for a while longer then he smiled at me like he realised something, his smile melts my heart, I feel like I want to touch him, kiss him and I have not felt like this about a guy in years.

"Hey, isn't this party and night meant to be for you? Why are you sitting here in a corner looking like baby?" Laughing I have to his baby comment is just too funny not to laugh at.

"Well, I would rather stay in the corner unlike baby, she has no choice, her daddy put her there, me I am happy here hiding. Considering the fact, I don't do all this, parties, people and things, I have not done it for years. My ideal night is watching TV and a glass of wine or any alcohol really. You can tell that seen as I only know Liam and Georgina here, I don't get out much" His laugh is perfect, his eyes are perfect, I feel drawn to him, my heart is quickening, what is happening to me? I need to sort my mind out, if I don't I will be hurt when he isn't interested which he isn't why would he be? I am too broken anyway, men would find out and run.

"Well, you should at least get to enjoy your birthday" He smiled, oh his smile I can't stop the image of me kissing his lips slipping into my mind, what am I doing? I have no chance, he is being friendly Alena, that is all friendly, my mind telling me to go for it, if Georgina isn't his type I certainly won't be.

"To be honest, I have to be at work for 10, so tonight would have been an early night" His hand reaches into his pocket, my eyes watching, catching a glimpse of his bulge, my eyes lock on it, what am I doing stop staring.

"I can walk you home if you like? It is nearly two" My eyes darting up to him, his phone in his hand. He winks at me, flip how can I say no to him? I should, he is Liam's brother and Georgina wants him yet at the same time I want to say yes, I should go home I really should I have work tomorrow.

"Okay, thank you, I will find Georgina and Liam and let them know I am leaving" He nods, standing up I walk towards the dance floor, Liam there dancing away, walking towards him his eyes catch me and he smiles.

"Alena, you finally came over to dance" His hand gripped my wrist, moving towards him, I should dance at least once with him. Dancing I look up, that look on his face, oh please don't kiss me, what the hell Liam. I shouldn't dance, stopping I look up at him, he is really going to kiss me, his hand still gripping my wrist, I can't do this.

"I am going home, I have work tomorrow and I am already shattered. Jackson has offered to walk me home, I hope you and Georgina enjoy the rest of your night though" I pull my arm away, he looks angry, but he isn't looking at me he is looking at Jackson, I don't want to cause trouble, especially not between him and Jackson.

"Fine, and yes, we will be home late" He turned, his face cold, he hates me, I know he does, maybe I should have been gentler about Jackson walking me home instead of just blurting it? He continues to dance, wow he isn't happy, I don't exactly want to face Georgina if she is going to react the same. I have told Liam, he will let her know so I don't need to go searching for her. Walking back to Jackson I smile at him, why does it make me happy that he is walking me home?

"All sorted, I am ready to go" He smiles at me, why do I feel so attracted to him?

"Come on then Kitten, let's get you home" Kitten really? Why did that word seem to turn me on? Walking out together we get stopped, Georgina standing here looking at us both, he walks by and stands at the entrance waiting for me.

"Where are you two going?" She looks at me, then looks at Jackson, she doesn't look happy at all, it is nearly two I made it past midnight that for me is amazing. However, I sense the not happy look is that I am leaving with Jackson, and he isn't staying here.

"I am going home, Jackson is going to walk me, remember I have work tomorrow, I will send him right back, don't worry" She looks worried though.

"Are you sure you want to do that Alena?" Have him walk me home, yes, he is Liam's brother and for some reason I feel I can trust him more than Liam. Walking past her, not answering or waiting for her objections I reach Jackson, smiling at me he grabs my arm linking it through his. Walking me home, maybe not such a great idea, while we live close to the centre, we live close to the university not the clubs. It will be a twenty-minute walk home, and my feet are already killing from dancing, but I am not going to complain, if I take them off I will be tiny next to him.

"So, Liam didn't look too happy that you were leaving" He didn't and I don't think it was the fact I am was leaving, more that I stopped him when he was about to kiss me.

"Yeah, I think they forget that all that isn't me anymore" He looked down to me, cocking his brow with clear questions on his mind.

"Anymore? So, you used to enjoy things like that before?" I can't deny it, I did, nodding I decide to answer.

"Yes, used too not anymore, things change, things happen and well, I never really feel comfortable anymore around people" I can see he has questions, but doesn't ask which I am grateful for. Reaching the apartment standing at the door, he stood in front of me, my body screaming for him to kiss me, I want him to kiss me, why can't I stop thinking about his lips on mine, my teeth bite down on my lip, looking at him, how can I feel so pulled to him?

"Well, it would be nice to be invited in for a quick drink. You know, to say thank you for walking you home and all" Nodding, I agree, unlocking the door, walking up to the apartment, walking in, I feel this electricity between us I can't ignore, it feels so weird.

"Erm, what do you want to drink?" I look at him, sat on my sofa, my sofa how did I manage to get him here and sitting on my sofa?

"Coffee if you have any" I walk back to the kettle and switch it on, talking to him from the kitchen, carrying his coffee to him, I sit down with him, my hairs standing up.

"So, you didn't drink much tonight?" My question aimed at him, as I noticed he hardly drank.

"I am not a big drinker, maybe once a twice, but not often, I prefer to keep a level head" Nodding, I understand that, but sometimes drinking can be the perfect way to hide the feelings.

"Anyway, how about university? You go there right, no friends or fellas?" Is that his way of asking if I am single without being outright about it?

"I have university friends, I call them that because once I leave university I don't really talk to them, as for fellas, not in a long time, too busy for that commitment" Okay, that last part is a lie, but I can't say the truth, the truth will make him run. He is looking at me like I have said something crazy, like me not having any men in a long time is just wrong. The cups now empty the room falls silent I can't stop thinking about his lips against mine, my heart begins to quicken feeling myself grow wet at the thought of him, what is going on with me? Grabbing the cups, I quickly stand up, escaping to the kitchen, I will wash them, then go back once I calm down I can't sit so close to him feeling like this. Standing here I feel the pull, he's behind me, good lord, how am I going to cope. How do I sense him so close to me so well? Turning to face him, he steps closer, my hairs standing up, my body screaming for him to touch me. I feel like a kitten in the gaze of a wolf. His body moves forward, without even a chance to think, his lips push against mine, so perfect, I can't stop myself, kissing back, I wrap my arms around his neck, pulling him to me, I need this, I need him, his kiss forceful yet amazing, struggling to breath I feel dizzy, he's making me dizzy. His hands cup my arse, lifting me onto the kitchen worktop. His arms grabbing my hair, pulling it, exposing my neck as his mouth starts to kiss down it, the moisture building between my legs, my hands run down his shoulders, what am I doing, my fingers unfastening him buttons, reaching the last one, my hands slide up his chest, my body screaming at the feel of him, pushing his shirt down over his shoulders. His growl loud, as his hands rip the dress open, it is falling down around my waist, his mouth kissing down, reaching my breasts slowly kissing them, his teeth gently biting down. My moans getting louder, my fingers unfastening his trousers, my hands sliding down inside, feeling his hard shaft, throwing my head back as his mouth keeps teasing down my body, my moans getting louder, this is not me at all, but I can't stop myself, I don't want to stop myself. My hand grabs his cock, slowly stroking it, feeling the hardness, making me more wet, my moans getting louder as his lips touch mine again, his arms wrapping around me, pulling me to him, wrapping my legs around him, feeling his cock push against my pussy, I moan. His hands grip my thong ripping it off me throwing it to the floor, the door swings open, looking up Georgina and Liam stand there, oh wow, please make a hole swallow me up, please, I am half naked with my legs wrapped around a guy in the kitchen with them two staring at us. Leaning against him, I try to hide my face and body, why would I do this here? The door to get in leads straight to the kitchen, the tensions so strong, Liam is glaring at Jackson, Georgina is ready to laugh. Please someone talk, anyone?

"You do realise I need to actually cook there right?" Not her, no, not her. Georgina's voice making me look up, her cook? None of us can cook, I would be laughing if I was not half naked, wrapped around a guy. Jackson starts to button up his trousers, his hands sliding up my arms, and pulling what is left of the dress up, lifting me down from the kitchen side, he leans down and grabs his shirt, he looked at me smiling.

"Don't look so embarrassed Alena, you should probably get a room next time, though" Georgina laughing at my face.

"No need, I should be leaving, and Alena needs sleep before work" He kissed my forehead and walked out, Liam chases after him, no doubt going to have an argument with him, warn him off and tell him to stay away.

"I want details, every single detail. I kind of wish we

had set off five minutes later, then we could have walked in at the really good part with you both fully naked" Rolling my eyes at her I shake my head.

"Why are you back anyway, Liam said you would be late?" They are back too soon, they can't have left long after us.

"Liam was all we need to go home, we need to check on Alena, we need to make sure she is okay, typical Liam bullshit" She shakes her head looking at me.

"Well, details" I was hoping my question would stop her thinking about that.

"I don't know what to say, I don't even know what happened, I just felt a pull to him, I escaped in here, using the cups needed to be washed as an excuse, then he was behind me, turning he grabbed me and kissed me, then you walked in" I can feel my pussy tightening thinking about it, why did I not go in the bedroom?

"Really? You skipped out the whole part of how you got on the side, how your dress got ripped, his shirt off and his pants open oh and apparently your thong ripped on the floor" Thinking back, I know how it happened, but at the same time it was like automatic, my mind just did it, I didn't think about what I was doing.

"All I know is I thought I should stop, but I couldn't I kept going my fingers unfastening his buttons, I touched his cock, I mean me, I actually touched it" I laughed this is not me, I have not been like this since before Max, but something about Jackson brought me back, he made me want to be how I used to be and open up.

"Well, I just hope Liam doesn't give him shit, I am pretty sure his plan was to kiss you tonight, like really sure he was going to Alena, I am surprised he didn't try before you left" I feel awful, really awful.

"He was going to at the club, I told him I was leaving with Jackson he looked pissed off, now I know for sure why. I don't see him in that way though, he's like a brother and to be honest he can be a prat at times and too much of a child" No matter what I can't see Liam as my partner, he is too close too much like a brother then anything.

"Well, tonight was fun, especially for you" She laughed, oh it was, and I knew tonight would cause trouble and clearly it has.

"Look, I am just going to go to bed, I have work soon. Say sorry to Liam for me, I really don't see him in that way, I don't want to hurt him either" Georgina looked at me like I was crazy, why am I crazy for pointing out he is not my type?

"You have nothing to apologise for, it isn't like you and Liam were dating or anything, or even had a history, seriously don't apologise" She is right, I don't have to apologise, yet I feel I should.

"Can you just explain to him, please, I will see you tomorrow, night" Hugging her good night, I turn walking to my room, letting my dress fall to the floor I look at my bed, the thought of what could have been happening right now flooding my mind, climbing in laying here I can't get the thought of him out my mind. His lips against my skin, kissing and teasing, my hand grabbing his shaft, the hardness that was for me. I feel like I should get up and go find him, sure I have no idea where to look, no idea at all but still the thought is in my mind to go find him. My eyes starting to close slowly as I get more tired and can't keep awake with the thoughts no more, my dirty thoughts turning into dreams. Waking up I feel tired, I slept yet the dreams were so vivid they kept waking me, jumping in the shower, hoping it clears my mind, but really doesn't, getting ready, I leave the bedroom, looking around, I can't see Liam, so I am guessing he is still in bed. The relief washing over me, it is not something I want to have to deal with before work. Grabbing a drink quickly and some food, I start making my way out the apartment, leaving for work, I should really drive I hardly ever use my car, there isn't much point me having it. Liam's car isn't here so it is clear I won't see him until tonight. Work is slow, my mind constantly on Jackson, on last night, it is replaying through my mind. I keep checking my phone every five minutes, why? He doesn't even have my number and I doubt Liam will give him it. Glad that it is time to leave, quickly packing up and rushing out like the others, I walk home. Getting in the apartment, I had hoped by now I would have somehow heard from Jackson, but now realisation has hit that it was more than likely just a one-night thing and he wouldn't be contacting me, sitting in the living room, hoping Liam comes home and Jackson has spoken to him, but I know it is unlikely. The issue was last night being on replay, constantly in my mind, over and over, I can't stop it no matter how much I try. I was a fool, a fool for thinking it would be more than a one-night stand, but then again, I am more annoyed with myself for not moving into the bedroom, at least then there would have been something good to remember, not just his lips on my body. Georgina walks through the door and in a way, I am glad, sure she was going to ask about Jackson and last night, but I won't be alone with these thoughts.

"How was work?" She smiles at me while turning the kettle on.

"Boring as usual, not much fun really" She always asks how work was, it is as if she is waiting for me to say it was amazing we danced on tables and everything, work is work boring and the same every day.

"Can I get some detail now about last night? Real details" Now she is asking I actually don't want her to I need to escape, talking about it will just make the memories worse.

"I am tired, I am going to go back to bed for a bit" Standing up and walking towards my room she stops me.

"So, no talking about Jackson or what happened last

night then? You realise it is only five O'clock right?"
She is pushing me and right now I can't handle it.

"Jackson? Really, there is nothing to talk about
Georgina, He was clearly after a one-night thing, he
never even asked for my number, let's be honest, I
had a lucky escape there, sure it would have been
nice too but then it would just be a mess, so no, I
don't see the point in talking about Jackson" She is
stood looking at me wide eyed, maybe I went too
far, but I don't really care right now, walking past
her, I climb into my bed, too worn out to even think
about anything, not even Jackson and his wicked
mouth came into my mind before my eyes closed.
Lips pressing against mine, I moan, they are kissing
me so passionately, his hands pulling me into him.
He starts ripping my clothes off, opening my eyes
Jackson was leaning over me, his lips pressing
against mine. He took my breath away, my
madness at him gone, all I want, all I need his him
again, the feel of his lips against my body. His lips
moved down, slowly kissing my neck, tilting my
head back to give him more room, my moans start,
his kisses moving down across my collar bone to my
breasts, gently sucking them in his mouth my moans
getting louder, his teeth bite down on my nipple
tugging them, my body pushing my breasts up
towards his mouth, begging him to play more. It
feels so amazing, I could stay here with him forever,
with him seducing me. His hands slowly began
pulling my trousers down, my hands unbuttoning

his shirt, pulling it off staring at his chest. The need to kiss it, I want to taste him, taste his body, laying here naked and entwined, every inch of my body is aching for him, his lips started kissing again over my naval, slowly down to my pubic bone, my back arching pushing up to his mouth. His tongue trailing down to my clit then to my pussy, my moans growing as his tongue begins teasing faster and harder, my hands gripping his hair, pushing him down, trying to make him go deeper, his tongue begins moving faster, harder, his fingers pushing inside my sex, moving slowly, moaning I can feel my orgasm rise, his tongue flicking over my clit with his fingers moving faster and harder deeper inside me, screaming I am on the edge of climaxing throwing my head back the orgasm rippling through my body, holding his head there still as the pleasure continued.

"Alena" I can hear Georgina's voice faintly in the distance, I don't care though, I don't want him to stop.

"Alena wake the hell up!" Jumping up, my eyes open, looking around I am in my room alone or at least without Jackson. Georgina is standing at the door looking at me. Please don't say I was moaning or screaming in my sleep, she is looking at me all serious.

"What now?" I am pissed, seriously pissed, that was the closet, I would ever get with Jackson and she just woke me up from it, I have never had a dream like it before.

"I had a text, we need to go to the hospital, Liam has been in a car accident, I don't know the details so get ready" Jumping out of bed, I grabbed any clothes on the floor I could see, adrenaline pumping through my veins, I will hate myself if anything bad has happened, I shot him down and the last memory I have is him looking hurt and angry over me and Jackson. I hope he is okay, the thought that he would hate me is not a good one, and I know he hates me. Running out the apartment the Taxi is waiting, we sit in silence, getting to the hospital, we run inside, going straight to the desk.

"We are here to see Liam Woodcock please"

"Are you family?" I look at her, she is annoying me already, what does that matter.

"No, we are his flatmates, we had a text about him being in a car accident" She raises her hand and points to seats behind us.

"I am sorry only family are allowed through, please take a seat and wait" Wow, really okay, I look at Georgina and she shrugs her shoulders, how do we even know he is okay? He could be laid through there dying, alone, I want to cry, I feel it building up inside, the thought that he could be so hurt, and we can't even see him. The door we came through opened, turning I see Jackson walking in, fear on his face, standing up, I look at him, he looks angry, he walks straight past, not even a word spoken, he blames me, he really does blame me, and I can't blame him, there is no way I can blame him for hating me when I am what caused them to fall out. Sitting back down all we can do is wait, Georgina's arm wraps around me, she smiles at me, but it doesn't help, that really hurts, he didn't even say Hi, it was like I was a ghost and he couldn't see me.

"It will be fine Alena, he is just worried about Liam, no doubt when he sees Liam is okay, he will talk to you" Georgina's voice quiet and soft, it doesn't help me at all, we don't even know if Liam is okay.

"I doubt it Georgina, just think, the last thing he and Liam did was argue over me, I caused them to fall out and we have no idea how bad Liam is, it is my fault" This is the exact reason I would not fight over a guy, it isn't worth it, it isn't worth hurting the other person yet while I was too consumed about Georgina I never thought of Liam. The door swung open, making a bang, Jackson stood there, his body rippling with anger, oh no, please don't say he has died, he has hasn't he and it is all my fault.

"What a bloody idiot, car accident, he says, no he ran over his foot, his own bloody foot, he knows how this would hurt my mum and did he care no, he thought it would be funny to say car accident" His body was shaking, his anger clear as anything. He looks scary, not the person I met that night at the club, yet at the same time there is so much pain in his eyes. Georgina begins laughing, everyone looking at her, I follow her eyes and see Liam at the door behind Jackson a cast on his foot.

"What sort of idiot runs over his own foot?" She is laughing so much at the state of him, yet Jackson just seems angry and rather annoyed now at Georgina for laughing at him.

"You should have said in the text you were okay, mum was in pieces when I left, it was like Katie all over again you idiot" Liam's face changed, he clearly understood what he had done, Jacksons face looks full of pain. Who is Katie?

"Sorry Bro, I didn't even think I just thought car accident sounded better than I ran over my own foot" Georgina against burst into laughter at Liam's excuse, Jackson looked angrier than before.

"If you think it is funny then you take him home, and when he is on his way make sure he calls my mum and apologises, properly none of this I thought it sounded cooler shit" Jackson turns looking at her waiting.

"Come on, hop along, let's get you home" She grabs Liam's arm to help him, turning to me she smiles.

"Let's just get him home Alena" Turning to walk with her, Jacksons hand grabs mine.

"I need to talk to Alena, so you can take him home yourself" Looking at him, I don't know if I want to, okay that is a lie I do want to, but should I? Turning to Georgina I nod, letting her know it is okay and to leave without me. She didn't argue or try to stop me, Liam however, doesn't look happy that I agreed to stay with Jackson, but I need to hear what he has to say. I can listen then walk away and not think about him again. Georgina and Liam walked out, looking at Jackson I wait for him to say something.

"Let's go to the pub, it is two minutes from here" Nodding in agreement, we walked to the pub, total silence why is he not saying anything? Looking at the clock it is nearly 4am, where the hell had Liam been? Sitting down by myself, he walked off to order our drinks, he came back sitting down and looking at me.

"I am not an arse, honestly, I am not the sort to fuck someone and run, not at all. I planned to come back, but well Liam got involved so I figured it was best to leave it" Wow, I should have known Liam would have had something to do with it, yet at the same time, I feel like I am missing so much and he isn't telling me the whole truth.

"He was meant to tell you that he warned me off, obviously he likes you Alena, I didn't want to cause trouble which is why I agreed to stay away if he told you" Obviously he didn't, I can't help but wonder why Liam would be so cruel, making me think he left without even wanting to talk to me again, like it was just a one night stand, and Jackson didn't care about me.

"Honestly Alena, about an hour before he text saying he had crashed, he text me saying he was going to pick you up from work and tell you" What the hell, Liam never picks me up from work.

"I don't work this late, so why he would say that I don't know. Plus, he never picks me up from work"

Why would he make out I was at work so late? It makes no sense; did he not think that I would find out?

"It might have been an excuse, I kept pushing him to tell you otherwise I was coming back, no doubt he said it as an excuse" Still doesn't make it right, he shouldn't have gotten involved.

"He text me then saying he had been in a car accident, my thoughts where you, I honestly thought you was in the car and fuck knows why but that scared me the thought of you being hurt. That is why I was, that way in the hospital, seeing you stood there obviously meant you wasn't in the car with him and he lied" His face showing pain, he was clearly scared for me and Liam, this has really shaken him up.

"I then prepared myself to see him messed up, I felt like it was my fault for wanting to fuck you, instead I saw him sat on the bed flirting with the nurses and laughing, that's why I got so angry" I have a feeling he's missing something out, but it has nothing to do with me, so I will stay quiet. I understand though, he is angry because he thought Liam was seriously hurt and turned out to be nothing. This conversation needs to change, I don't want to spend the time talking about Liam.

"So, you said you own your own businesses, what are they?" His smile was so tempting.

"Well, that is for another time, not something I discuss with people until I know how they will take it" Smiling, I can't help but wonder what it is, my mind telling me loads of different businesses that he might possibly own, Liam will know as much as I am pissed off with him for this, he owes me so can tell me.

"Don't even think about Liam, he doesn't know, it isn't often we see each other, and my business is no concern of his" Is he a mind reader, how would he think to cover that? Okay, so business talk is off the table, what else is there to talk about?

"So, where exactly do you live?" I can't help but ask, something makes me want to know.

"Not far from here, about 10 minutes' drive, why?" He is looking at me like he's trying to assess why I would ask, why did I ask? Why do I feel like I want to go to his house? My mind flooded with images of the other night biting my lip I need to try to sort myself out.

"I was just wondering if you live alone and get some privacy?" Well, there it is, me trying to invite myself to his house, if he lives alone, then that would be amazing no awkward interruptions halfway through our shenanigans. His eyes stayed locked on mine, my mind replaying the kitchen slowly, my heart racing, getting louder. He starts to stand up, his hand grabbing mine pulling me from the seat, taking his key out he began to lead me outside. Am I really going to do this, it isn't me, sure it used to be but not anymore. Walking through a small alleyway towards the car park my mind screaming at me to do something, kiss him anything. I need to get out of here the space is too tight, pushing me closer to him, to close for me to concentrate. He turns, his hands gripping my wrists, pushing my back against the wall, his mouth kissing mine, pinning my arms above my head, a moan escaping my lips as he pushed against me more, the feel of his shaft beneath his trousers. Letting go, he carried on walking, a little faster than before to get us to his car. Driving in silence, I watched as we got out the town centre, surrounded by trees and fields we pulled into a drive, the whole place beautiful and open. The house was breathtaking, I have only seen houses like this in magazines and on TV, walking in it is even more beautiful than outside, the place covered in windows, looking out over the trees and fields it was natural and beautiful. The size of the entrance bigger than my whole apartment. Leading me inside, we walk to the kitchen.

"Do you want alcohol, hot drink or something else?" Looking at him was he serious about alcohol.

"It's a little too early for alcohol, so I will stick with a can of coke if you have any?" Watching him walk to the fridge, he opened it, taking out a can of coke, walking towards me he hands me the drink, walking around his kitchen, looking outside it is beautiful, I can't stop looking it is as good as being outside, the windows full length. I almost forgot I was here, he stepped in front of me, his body pinning me against the kitchen worktop. Instantly my body screaming for him, his hand cupped my chin, lifting my face up, my eyes meeting his and he gazed into my eyes. My heart is pounding fast already, his face slowly moving closer and closer to mine, suddenly his lips on mine, we begin kissing, his lips are so soft, he tastes so sweet. I can't control myself, my hands want to explore his body, running up his chest, feeling his body beneath the shirt, the more I touch the stronger the need to touch him is. Why do I feel like I have missed him? I don't even know him, yet I feel like I have known him for ages and he's been out of my life for years. I can't stop myself, my fingers start to unbutton his shirt, feeling the warmth of his skin beneath it, the more I touch the less control I have, I am losing control of myself and I love it. Finally, his buttons are all unfastened, my hands running up his torso to his shoulders, a slight moan escaping my lips as I do, pushing his shirt down, watching it fall to the floor. His hand wraps around my waist, his kiss more forceful, lifting me up onto the worktop, moaning from the pleasure of his hands touching me. My hands move down, slowly stroking his body, unbuttoning his trousers, his hands grabbing mine, I begin frowning at him for stopping me. His hands pull my top off, his lips back on mine, my hands unfastening his trousers again, moaning against his lips, pulling his trousers down, his shaft now free I can't stop the gasp from my mouth, I had felt it last time, I knew it was big, but I was not expecting it to be this big. My body shook all over, I grasp his cock in my hand, as he unfastens my bra, throwing it on the floor, my hand teasing, stroking his cock moaning against his lips, the feel of his shaft throbbing in my hand. His hand pushes against me, my body falling back onto the kitchen side, his lips kissing around my navel, my moans getting louder, my hands grasping his hair, needing and wanting more. His hands gripping mine, standing up, his cock pushing against my sex as his head lowers kissing my breasts, my legs wrapping around him, trying to pull him to me. His shaft pushing against my trousers, damn things in the way, I am losing my mind, but I can't stop myself from wanting him. His hands unwrapping my legs from around him, trailing back up to my breasts, squeezing them, then moving back down, his hand pulling my trousers and underwear down, dropping them on the floor. My breathing gets faster, my body begging for him to fuck me, right here on the worktop. His tongue flicked over my hip, slowly kissing down till he reached in between my legs, my sex already wet from excitement, his mouth kissing gently, his tongue slowly stroking my pussy. My moans getting louder as he teases, his tongue quickly flicking over my sex, my hands grasping his hair again, trying to keep him between my legs, my orgasm rising, I can feel myself falling apart right now under his touch, his tongue teased around my clit, slowly licking it, my back arching my moans getting louder, I want so much more. His tongue moving down, pushing inside my aching pussy, I can feel myself getting to the limit, his fingers rubbing against my clit, and tapping it, the sensation is phenomenal. I have never experienced anything like it, my back arching more, his name escaping my lips, my body closing, getting closer to the orgasm, my moans getting louder, his tongue pushing in and out of my throbbing pussy, his fingers moving faster over my clit, my moans now turning into screams, I can't control this, my body letting me orgasm, my hands pulling hard on his hair, the feel of my juices running free. He dragged me off the side, he looks so different, gasping for air as he spins me around, pushing my chest down against the worktop, moaning from the feel, his hands holding me there, I can feel his legs pushing mine open. His shaft pushing against my core, moaning I try to push back on it, wanting him to give me the full length. He thrust hard, pushing himself inside of me, screaming, I try to get up, I want to move closer to him, his hand, though pinning me down, I love it and for some reason I want more. His hips slowly moving building up a rhythm, thrusting in and out of me, his other hand gently massaging my butt, turning my legs to jelly my whole-body tingling. A sharp sting across my ass, my screams escaping, legs giving away from the spank, his hips pounding fast and hard, my body getting closer to an orgasm, his hips pushing harder with each thrust, my own screams turning to whimpers as I feel my body begging for a release, his hand moved rubbing up and around my neck, choking me he pulled me upright. He has his hand at the perfect angle, I can breathe yet still feel the pain and pleasure. My body now moving against his, my hips grinder against him, it is pointless though, his hips are thrusting so fast and hard mine barely makes a difference, his hand still on my throat, his other hand grabs one of my breasts, sending me over the edge, my body giving away as the orgasm took control. He keeps pounding hard and fast, his own moans growing as he is nearly reaching the point to climax as well, his moan loud as he gave a last thrust, the feel of him throbbing inside of me. He moved back, removing his shaft from inside me, going to let go, he stopped noticing my body was going to fall. Pulling me to the floor, we lay panting, out of breath and sweaty. His hand stroked up and down my body, I can feel that he was still shaking with pleasure.

"You can't beat a morning fuck" Jacksons voice quiet breaking the silence, turning to him laughing, trying to steady my breathing.

"I agree" I do, I feel amazing right now, admiring his body, I notice a tattoo, a small footprint wrapped in a blanket, I would love to know what it means but right now isn't the right time for personal questions. Lying here my breathing begins to return to normal, replaying what just happened in my mind, it was unexpected yet amazing, he seems like a totally different person before we had sex. I can't remember ever feeling so much enjoyment from a man before, I have to admit I love the fact that he controlled whether I could move or not. I have experienced it before, but it was not a good controlling before this time it was, most of my partners have asked me what I wanted and then let me take charge, it feels amazing that he took charge and pleasured me in ways I have never been pleasured before.

"Well, we can't just lie on the kitchen floor all day, I am going to jump in the shower. Want to join me or will you be showering alone?" He was being playful, his hands gently tickling me, I would love to get in the shower with him, but I honestly don't think I can handle anymore sex just yet, I know that will happen if I agree and I still feel like jelly. I'm not used to being fucked like that, all of the men I slept with seem so tame compared to Jackson. I feel so self-conscious as well right now, like I should cover my body and hide.

"I think I will get in on my own, I don't think us sharing a shower would be a good thing right now, I need time to recuperate" Laughing hoping he understood. He laughed back, nodding clearly agreeing and understanding what I mean. His laugh is so cute, yet so manly how is that even possible?

"Okay, give me two minutes, I will grab you a robe to put on" He jumped up, fully naked, my eyes following him, trying to force my eyes to look elsewhere I just failed. How did I manage to get him? Sitting up looking around for the first time I feel uneasy, just realising that we have been fucking in front of a window, a window that is not covered in any way. I hope no one decided to take a stroll and see us, I can feel my face getting red at the thought, the embarrassment of someone seeing us and possibly watching as well, Jackson walks back down the stairs, carrying a robe, he handed it to me. "I will jump in now, make yourself at home, the living room is through there. No snooping though" He points towards a door, clearly not needing to the room was all windows you can see the sofa and that it is a living room easy, he walked back upstairs, looking around I noticed a few other doors where the room was hidden by walls unlike the living room. It would be wrong to snoop wouldn't it? Of course, it would, I am guessing the one in the kitchen is probably a closet, walking towards the living my mind reminds me, I have not spoken to Georgina since before I left, I should really check my phone. Walking back towards the kitchen I can't seem to see my coat, walking towards the entrance I can see it in the hall, grabbing my coat I check the pockets, taking out the phone. My eyes looking up seeing another door, slightly jarred open, no harm peeking if it was already open right? Walking towards it, looking in, it was clearly an office, but the fact I know nothing about his business is making it tempting to go inside and look. There is no harm, just walk around to see if anything is lying around that gives an idea of what his businesses are, then maybe I can work out what they are, foolish I know walking inside, I plan to skim over any documents I might see. Walking around the office, I am shocked there is none, not a single document, what sort of man keeps his office so tidy and not a single piece of paperwork left out?

"What did I say about snooping?" Jumping I spin to look at him, Jackson stood at the door, water dripping down his perfect body, my breathing stopping, I need to breath, but he is stopping me just from standing there. I can't not smile, a blush showing on my face, I can feel the warmth, looking at him realising now he looks displeased with me, I need an excuse, phone in hand I have one.

"I am just trying to find a charger, my phone died, and Georgina has probably sent out a search part by now, no snooping honestly" Lie I know, but I hope I sound genuine, he stays looking at me for a few more seconds, then seems to believe me, walking into the office, he opened a draw pulling out a cable and handing me it.

"You can either plug it in here or in the living room, it is up to you, I will show you where the shower is" He points to the corner where the socket is, of course it is going to be plugged in here, I would have another chance to snoop later, I never learn ever, plugging it in I begin to follow him upstairs, my eyes peering at his towel, my mind now hoping it will fall off, why do I want sex already again? He carries on walking, into a room.

"Shower is there, easy to figure out, there is a towel hung up there as well" Standing I find myself staring at him, please just pounce on me like before, my mind going crazy wanting him to do it. Yet he doesn't seem to be thinking about it, or if he is, he is trying to be the gentleman and not pounce on me after I said no.

"I'll bring your clothes up and put them on the side for you" He turns walking out, stepping into the shower just standing, my mind clearing of all the thoughts as the water runs down my body, it feels so relaxing, my mind empty, then images of Jackson and downstairs coming back, mixing with the shower, my mind showing me what could have been happening right now had I agreed to shower with him. I can't believe I just fucked a guy I basically don't know in his kitchen, what the hell is it with kitchens? Is that a me thing or a him thing? Quickly washing I step out the shower, getting dried, I pick up my clothes, what the hell had I put on I look a mess. Realising he had brought up the clothes I had not even heard him come in with them, walking downstairs slowly I turn to face the kitchen, my body freezing, Jackson stood there with just jogging bottoms on, moping the kitchen floor. Standing here ogling him, just gazing at him in amazement, the sides have clearly been cleaned, as they look wet. Wow, it is hard not to stare at him.

"Are you enjoying staring at me?" His voice quiet, my body jumping from the shock how does he know, he's facing the other way.

"I can see your reflection in the window" Can he read minds? He keeps answering my silent questions, maybe my mind is just that predictable he can guess what I am thinking?

"Ah, I was just admiring your tattoos, I was too intoxicated to notice them before" I hadn't noticed them, sure I knew he had tattoos but never took them in fully.

"Too intoxicated? Are you sure you weren't just too mesmerised by my hot body to notice?" He is teasing, and slightly big headed to be honest.

"Well, I guess you could say that, but, I prefer the word intoxicated honestly rather than mesmerised" I start to laugh, walking towards him, as I did, he turns around there are more tattoos on his chest. They make me feel weak, my hands wanting to rub across his body, touching each one.

"What are you wearing anyway? I am slightly lost by your style right now" he laughs looking at me, and I don't blame him at all.

"I was asleep, I don't wear clothes to bed often, Georgina woke me about Liam, I grab the first items of clothing I could find, the end result is well this" Laughing I can't believe what I have on, sweats that are thin and old, and a baggy t-shirt, he nods laughing at my response.

"Georgina rang while you were showering" My eyes

flicked up to him, he answered my phone? Who does that seriously?

"You answered my phone?" My words accusing him, why had I just accused him instantly? He looks shocked that I would accuse him, that was wrong, even if he did answer my phone, no doubt he only did it because it said Georgina on the screen, my words sounded cold.

"No, I didn't, Liam rang me because Georgina was freaking out that you weren't answering, she got on the phone. I tell you not to snoop and you do then accuse me of answering your phone?" His words quick, not hurtful just confused, I feel like shit now, I am not like this, or wasn't it is all down to Max.

"Sorry, that was wrong of me to accuse you, and assume you did it, the past is not always easy to forget and move on from, I shouldn't have accused you. I am guessing she wants to know when I am going home?" I hope he takes my apology, I feel awful, I have enjoyed my small time with him, he makes me want to live life again.

"Yes, she was going on and on about Liam annoying her, she can't cope anymore on her own with him, but that doesn't matter what about your past?" He looks at me waiting, this is not something I am willing to go into when I just met a guy, maybe if things get serious sure, but right now no. I know he is probably walking away after today anyway, but me reveling my past will make him run not walk.

"Nothing important right now, it can wait for

another day just like your business" Smiling at him, reminding him he was not willing to talk about his business to me.

"Okay, grab your phone, I better run you home before Liam ends up back in the hospital by Georgina's hands, maybe we should tell Liam about this morning?" His question obviously only has one answer, I live with Liam I can't not tell him, Jackson is his brother but at the same time I know this is going to cause some crap, he had freaked out the other night, and I feel awful for what I did, actually, felt awful because then he told Jackson to leave and lied to me and didn't care how it would hurt me.

"It is up to you, I don't think it has anything to do with him, but he is your brother, which matters more than him being my flatmate, so I will let you decide" Out of my hands, I am not choosing to lie to him, neither am I choosing to hurt him by telling him, Jackson is. Grabbing my things, I followed him out to the car, something tells me that is was a one off and won't happen again. Maybe that is it, after he drops me home, he is telling Liam and going? Why is my mind so set on thinking it is a one-night stand without proof? My mind telling me that I am not good enough, not worthy of a man like him, he said he was not the kind of guy to do it, maybe though he is, the drive was long, or seems it because we aren't talking, all the possibilities running around in my head. What do you talk about after sleeping with a guy you barely know anyway?

He said he thought I was in the car and he was worried for me, why? Why was he so bothered about me, someone he doesn't even know? My anxiety is getting worse, the longer the silence lasts the worse I feel. This is Max, he made me think no man would be interested, and now I believe it, I don't feel worthy yet something about Jackson makes me feel alive again. Pulling up to the house, I get out, walking a little too fast. Walking straight upstairs with him right behind me, he doesn't say anything, just follows, walking into the apartment Georgina flew at me.

"Don't you dare leave me alone with wonky donkey again, ever. Where were you and what the hell was you doing anyway? Wait did you have a shower, seriously?" I can't do this right now, shaking my head at her I turn, her questions will only make Liam start as well.

"I need a drink anyone else?" Walking past her I open the fridge hoping that she would realise I was trying to avoid her questions.

"Sure, I am dying of thirst, Georgina isn't exactly a great nurse" Liam's voice travelling from the living room, Georgina's eyes still staring at me, I hope she will just leave it, I don't want to get into things in front of Liam, she realises finally smiling at me.

"Coffee please" She sits down on a stool watching me. Walking to the kettle I glance at Jackson, waiting for him to reply, this is it, if he says no it means it was nothing. Maybe that is best, if I am that worked up about him already, how much of a mess would I be in a few weeks when he leaves for someone like Georgina?

"I suppose I have time for a coffee, thanks" He looks undivided, sighing I grab the cups, at least he isn't running straight away. Jackson walks towards the living room, sitting next to Liam, Georgina's eyes on me, waiting she has clearly got so many questions.

"So, did you tell her to stay away?" Liam's voice quiet, yet I can hear him, his eyes glance towards me, obviously not realising I can hear, trying not to make it look like I can hear him, I carry on, he looks pissed off though.

"Seriously, no I didn't Liam, what did you expect? You lied to me, you were going to let her think I was a piece of shit and just wanted a quick fuck then move on, yeah, I told her that you told me to stay away, don't try to make me look like a dick" Jackson seems so calm, his voice low yet I can sense he is annoyed with Liam, he sounds mad, calm but mad.

"You knew I liked her, I made you look like a dick for a reason, so then maybe, just maybe she would be interested in me" Liam's explanation just makes me angry, is he for real? Clearly, it has annoyed Jackson as well, as he is now looking angry.

"I'm not walking away Liam, I won't be walking away at all, if anything, you just pushed me into wanting her more and wanting to stay around her" Jackson voice quiet, angry yet his words making me smile, relief floods through me that he wanted more. I feel like it is a trick, my mind reminding me of Max his words was he right?

"You don't care about her at all, you wanted a fuck and now you're going to move on, like you do I know you will, are you forgetting just how many women I have seen you with before Caroline?" Liam's voice loud, he seems to have forgotten that we are here, Georgina is looking concerned, Jackson stands up, his body towering over Liam, while he clearly intimidating, he didn't seem like the sort to hit Liam, I feel like I should stop him, but I feel frozen to this spot, they are brothers, no doubt they argue all the time, Georgina's arm nudging me, I am not getting involved. The hostility reminds me of the past, something I never wanted to experience again, yet this is different, but it still has me on edge.

"Why is Jackson so defensive over you Alena?" Looking at her, her eyes look into mine, but I don't know how to respond I have no idea, turning back, I look at Jackson and Liam, just make up and sort your shit out please.

"I've fucked her already, I will fuck her again, whether you like it or not Liam, it is happening get used to it, if it was just a fuck I would have dropped her off and not came in" Georgina's gasp loud, I can feel her eyes on me, everyone now looking at me, everyone, even Jackson realises how loud he had said it, frozen and embarrassed explains me right now, frozen to the spot, Liam looking at me, his eyes begging me to walk away from Jackson, like he wants me to tell him he is wrong and I just wanted a one night thing. Jackson looks at me waiting for me to confirm what he has said, like he wants me to say yes, now it is serious. Can everyone stop staring at me? Seriously feel like I am dying inside yet everyone is staring at me.

"You two were not dating, ever you have never done anything like that. It is not like she is your ex, or your partner, I wouldn't do that to you Liam, but to say I can't go near any woman you like is ridiculous" Jackson has a point, if everyone said who they liked were off limits the world would cease to exist.

"Why are you even here? We spoke about this the other night, you promised to leave her alone, so clearly she didn't mean that much to you, you don't even know her, but you knew I liked her and you went behind my back anyway" Liam looks hurt, I feel awful, but worse I feel humiliated by this whole thing.

"I only agreed to walk if you explained to her why, maybe if you actually told her that you told me to stay away this wouldn't have happened, you didn't though, instead you just made me look like a dick, let's be honest Liam, you didn't say anything because you wanted her to hate me so she wouldn't want me" Jackson retorted, I feel my face growing red, the anger rising inside me, why are they doing this, they are acting like I am not here, like I don't exist and like they both own me.

"HEY! I AM HERE YOU KNOW" My own voice now shouting loud and shocking me. They are both bloody idiots both acting like I was an object fighting over me, fighting over who should have me and what I should be told.

"Honestly, you two, I get your brothers, but you're just as bad as each other. You are both talking about me like you own me, nobody owns me, you can't tell people to stay away from me either" I looked at Liam pointing my finger.

"You lied to me Liam, you made me feel like crap, why? So you could get into my bed, see you're just as bad you say he doesn't care about me, clearly you don't either, you're both idiots, not one of you thought of me while you made your little deal" I can't deal with them, walking out the kitchen I go into my bedroom, my door slamming behind me, what the hell was going on, sure I knew there would be problems with them being brothers, but I never once expected them to sit and discuss me like an object they own. I feel awful, tears begin to gather in my eyes, biting my lip to stop myself from crying, do they not have any respect at all? I have no feelings for Liam, at all no matter what I won't. He's like a brother to me, with Jackson though, I feel a magnet like it is forcing us together, I can't stop thinking about him. He has changed me, just like that a flip switched and I found the old me, and that is down to him. I know I made this mess, but I never told Liam I had feelings for him, I have never led him on or made out I liked him. It's complicated, this is all because I went out for my birthday, had I just skipped it again this year, things would be normal, okay and not a mess. Then again, had I skipped it, I would still be sat in my room hating life and not wanting to live it. I can't ruin their relationship with each other, I can't stay living here with Liam, if there is a chance I will bump into Jackson, I need to walk from them both. The sound of a knock at the door, making me look towards it.

"Let me in" Georgina's voice quiet, moving I unlocked the door, letting her walk in. She walked in sitting on my bed, not saying anything.

"You really did cause some crap this weekend, didn't you? At least it'll be a birthday to remember" She is laughing, trying to make a joke out of it.

"I know, alright. On the night of my birthday, I should have said no to him walking me home, I even thought to myself that it was stupid, with him being Liam's brother. I don't know what it is about him, though, something draws me to him and I don't even know him. I know Liam's annoyed at me, and I can't say that I blame him, it's entirely my fault" Explaining to her, I realise I need to walk away from them both.

"Alena, don't even think about walking away from Jackson because of Liam, I have not seen you confront someone like that in years, he is good for you" She is right, but I can't carry on knowing I am destroying their relationship.

"It is my fault, the fact they have fallen out and hate each other. I can't be with Jackson knowing it is making them argue" I hate seeing Liam so hurt by all of this.

"You do realise what they're doing right now don't you? They are sitting together playing on a new game, arguing over that now. They are brothers, they make up quicker than sister do, especially when they need an extra player for a game" Georgina laughing at least they were not killing each other. As relieved as I am, I can't help but feel like I should still call it off, not see Jackson anymore and just move out, it makes me feel sad thinking about it, but maybe it is the best.

"Look, the worse thing was Liam, right? What can be worse than Liam finding out, nothing, so just relax the worse is over, enjoy whatever you and Jackson have" She is right, I should just get on with it, Liam is one of my closest friends and I wouldn't want to hurt him, so I hope he can get used to the idea. The worst thing while she thinks it is Liam, I know different, it is Max getting over him that is the worst part and having to tell Jackson about him as well. Now I just feel foolish for my outburst, I must have looked like a five-year-old throwing a tantrum. How am I supposed to show my face in there now? I don't really have a choice, I have to leave at some point, Georgina walking to me, pulling me up.

"Come on Alena, let's go back in there" She began

dragging me to the door. It was easier than I thought, they barely even looked up as we entered, they are to engross in their game shouting at each other for being rubbish and letting the other die, the day passed quickly, I spent so much time with my eyes on Jackson, just looking at him, kind of like a stalker would. My body is tired, my eyes, wanting to close. The events of this weekend, and lack of sleep have left me feeling exhausted, I have university in the morning, so I definitely need an early night tonight.

"Well, I better get moving, I have things to do tomorrow and I need to plan them properly tonight. I'll see you later bro" Jackson stood up, kicking Liam's bad foot, Liam's scream loud showing the pain it caused.

"That is for being a pain in the arse, making us all think you were dying in a car accident" He laughed walking away from Liam towards me and Georgina. My heart pounding fast, I hope no one can hear it, I swear I can.

"Bye Georgina, I will no doubt be seeing you again at some point" He laughed, she smiled, walking off and sitting with Liam, leaving him stood alone with me, I can feel the magnet pulling me towards him, his head leaning down, kissing me. It is soft and passionate, my hands wrapping around his neck, pulling him to me, Christ Alena, get a grip and stop. The urge to rip his clothes off showing, his lips slowly kissing along my jaw, biting my lip to try to stop myself moaning, he stops at my ear whispering.

"I will find you tomorrow, so don't be too surprised if I just turn up" His breath against my ear, sending shivers down my spine, turning he walked towards the door, opening it to leave.

"Wait, you're going tomorrow right? Same time as always?" Liam asks his question as he hobbled towards me passing me and going to Jackson.

"Yes, I always do. I'll be taking mum with me, so you can either meet us there or come to mums first" Jackson whispered back yet sitting here I was purposely trying to hear and grateful I can.

"Does she now know yet? You do realise you're going to have to tell her at some point, right?" Liam whispered back, my mind wondering what they were talking about.

"Let's not start another argument again, no one needs to know anything right now, so keep it shut" Jackson turned, walking out, not giving Liam a chance to reply, my mind throwing everything at me that could be a possibility of what they were speaking about. I could easily ask Liam, but that wouldn't be right, and I can't deal with him now either.

"I am off to bed, I'm exhausted, I will see you tomorrow. Liam I am really sorry I didn't mean to hurt you" Even after everything I still feel the need to apologise, all he could do was grunt back, Georgina hugged me.

"When are you telling him about Max?" Seriously, I would rather wait as long as I can before mentioning him.

"There is no need for him to know, not yet anyway" I don't think there is maybe I am wrong though?

"Alena, this isn't something you can hide, Max left marks, scars and damage that no doubt will soon catch up and cause trouble if Jackson doesn't know" She is right, but I don't care, I am not ready to tell him my story yet. Nodding, I slowly begin walking to my bedroom, I climb into bed, my eyes closing quickly, and sleep, taking me away just as quick, no thoughts of Jackson, Max or Liam in my mind, no replays of my past.

2 SECRETS DON'T STAY HIDDEN

The ringing of the alarm waking me, I could just fall back to sleep, I really could, I still feel exhausted, but today is going to be a good day, why wouldn't it be, after all Liam now knows and that is sorted, kind of. Hopefully I get to see Jackson, I am looking forward to that. Opening my bedroom door to leave, Liam's voice came through, peeking out I can see him on the phone, staying quiet I try to listen to what he is saying. This feels wrong on so many levels, but I can't not listen, especially if he is talking about what ever last night's conversation was about.

"Listen, Jack, you will have to tell her at some point, it's not a secret you can keep from someone you're planning on spending a lot of time with, has she not even questioned the tattoos yet, I won't let you bullshit her and not tell her the truth" There was a pause while this Jack was replying, who is he talking to?

"Whatever Jackson, she needs to know about Katie, and Tallulah, I never mentioned Katie why would I it was before I met her, if you don't I will tell her myself" He removed the phone from his ear, ending the call. Jack is Jackson, shutting the door quietly, walking and sitting on the bed, I feel awful, who the hell is Tallulah and Katie, is this what today is about the place they are going. Jackson mentioned Katie at the hospital before. Every thought possible in my mind, he's married, he has a girlfriend, something doesn't feel right, and to be honest, now I want to walk, to Liam whatever it is, it is important I know. That alone makes me wonder what he is hiding and why, I need to know, but I can't ask Liam he will know I was listening, grabbing my things I head out of my room, Liam nowhere in sight, I am grateful for that, leaving quickly I walk to university. I know now that today isn't going to be that great, something tells me it is just going to get worse, the only thoughts in my mind is Jackson and who these two names relate to. I shouldn't care, we have only just met, but the last thing I want is getting closer to him if he is married, or has a girlfriend already, something isn't right. Trying to concentrate on classes is unavailing all that is in my mind is Jackson, I need a drink, something to help process the thoughts and slow them down, I need to find a way to think clearly and resolve this, walking out I get to the bar, sitting there for a while drinking alone, I am not in the mood to be around people. Actually, when am I ever in the right mood to be around people? Students are looking at me strange, I never come alone, actually I hardly ever come at all and usually I am with Georgina. The thoughts still lingering in my mind, each one battling for the stand, the whole thing making me feel worse. My mobile ringing looking down, now realising the time it was 8:15pm I have been sitting in here for hours. I should answer, but I want to be alone with my thoughts right now, I have cancelled so many calls from Georgina sat here.

"Hello?" I answer trying to sound normal and failing. "Where the hell are you? Georgina said you should have been home over four hours ago, what's going on?" Wow, Jackson voice full of worry, what the hell is he ringing me for, and what has it to do with him where I am and if I am not home when I was meant to.

"I'm at the student bar, I didn't know I'd have to constantly update you on where I am, if this is the sort of guy you are, sorry, but no I won't do it, been there before and I have no plans to go back" Max flashes in my mind, hanging up the phone, my hand shaking, Jackson does not seem like Max at all, yet something about him and his secrets have me on edge, a lot. Flashbacks from Max on my mind, a pass I want to run from, yet it always catches back up to me and drags me down. I was too harsh to Jackson, he asked a simple question, he didn't shout, he wasn't angry more worried, gabbing another drink, I sit down, the thoughts in my mind worse than before, I guess I will need to go home soon and face everyone.

"You really have an attitude sometimes, don't you?" Jumping at the sound of Jacksons voice from behind me, I feel sick, he walked around, sitting opposite me, his eyes just looking at me, trying to assess me, waiting I want to see if he is going to tell me about the two women, but I don't think he will be.

"Look, sorry for ringing and sounding like I am stalking you, you weren't home I was fine waiting. Georgina said you always go straight home, then she was rambling on about hoping you had not been found by someone and she should call you, then it kept cutting out" He is looking at me, like he wants me to explain. Why would Georgina say that? Does she not realise it is my past, and only mine to tell?

"Yes, okay, I was out of order demanding to know where you were, I am sorry something just makes me want to protect you, I don't know why and when she mentioned being tracked down I panicked, what did she mean?" He stayed looking at me, maybe I should tell him, but if I am, I want to know about Katie and Tallulah first.

"I don't know, maybe you could tell me who Katie and Tallulah are?" The thoughts are coming back, my body getting ready to get up and walk away, his face changed, he looked hurt, his face full of sadness, what the hell is going on?

"What has Liam told you? He can't keep his mouth shut, I told him there was no need for you to know" Something tells me that I am wrong about it, but at the same time my mind is telling me I am a fool for thinking he isn't seeing anyone else.

"Liam has not said anything, not to me anyway. He needs to learn to take private calls somewhere no one can hear him, if you seem to think there is no need for me to know about these two names, then I guess you don't need to know what Georgina was talking about either" he can't ask me to tell him something, but then not tell me what is going on with his side, this whole thing is messed up, if it is like this now how bad will it be in a few months?

"Fine, I'll tell you, but then I want to know what Georgina was talking about, okay? He looked at me waiting, I nod in agreement.

"Look, if we want this to work, then maybe it's a good thing being open with each other this early on. We both have pasts that are pushing forward and trying to push us apart, if we are honest, we can decide then if we stay or walk, at least then in two or three months we can't say well we didn't know the truth because we will" He sounds genuine, nodding in agreement.

"Okay, go ahead, you start" I brace myself for the hurt to follow, the hurt my mind has been telling me will happen all day, girlfriends, wife? What else could it be?

"Okay, so Tallulah is my daughter, Katie, is our little sister, the reason I have not mentioned them, and Liam obviously never has mentioned them is because they both died" Oh shit, I feel like a bitch, a total bitch, my blood running cold at the thought.

"My ex, Caroline and I had a beautiful girl, she was born on Katies birthday, however, she was born early and didn't take her first breath. Caroline didn't cope well, one night she and Katie were out in the car, she drove straight into a wall, Katie died instantly, no one has seen Caroline since" He looks hurt, I want to comfort him, and I now get why he flipped at Liam, Christ I would have if I knew, why say he has been in a car accident knowing his sister died in one?

"I am sorry" His hand lifted, his finger on my mouth to keep me from talking.

"We visited the graves today, it is their birthday. So, there you go. You can see now why I didn't want you to know just yet, it is not the sort of thing you tell someone straight away"

"I am so, so sorry, I shouldn't have pushed you into telling me, it was just the way Liam had said things on the phone made it sound wrong. Is that tattoo for Tallulah?" I had to ask, the footprint in my mind.

"The tattoo is of Tallulah's foot print, wrapped in a blanket, the blanket that was Katie's since she was a baby, she gave it to Tallulah, she was buried wrapped in it" Fighting back tears I nod, why am I such an idiot sometimes?

"So, go on it's your turn, and you can't say it doesn't matter" He looks at me, waiting how do you talk about something you never speak of, something you try to hide from and never want to think about. I can feel my whole body turning cold, starting to shiver, I don't even know if I can, I look up at him, sitting there waiting, where do I start I can't even find the words. The feel of a tear running down my cheek, my frustration building, he stays sat quiet waiting, clearly able to see that I was fighting a battle in my own mind.

"I was engaged to someone, he wasn't a nice person at all, and the relationship got to the point where he had my phone, he checked any calls and texts before I did, when I answered calls it had to be on the loudspeaker. I couldn't go out anywhere, eventually I couldn't even go to university without him" Taking a break, I have a drink, his eyes still on me.

"He'd accuse me of things, it got to the point I was not allowed my phone, I couldn't leave the apartment, I never saw family or friends. One night I ran, going to Georgina's she drove us here, we stayed in a hospital until we found the apartment. That is why I flipped when I thought you answered my phone, and why I freaked out by you demanding to know where I was" I can't tell him the details, I can't go into that much without breaking down.

"Did anything else happen?" He asked, pushing for

more information, but I can't give him it yet.

"No, what now then, are you going to run away?" I would be shocked if he didn't to be honest, I have not exactly been nice towards him.

"No, why would I? I do think though that maybe I am not the best person for you, but we both have pasts which we tried to hide, failed at and well now we both know about them. We do need to talk more about it though, as I am sure you have questions for me just like I do with you"

"I honestly would not have asked where you were or acted like I did today, Georgina looked scared for you, she wound me up going on and on about it, I still don't understand why she would think you would be tracked down?" He had no forgot, clearly, I was going to have to answer.

"He was locked up, but kept trying to reach me, he said he'd find me when he was released" Explaining, it was like Max's voice in my mind, his face there plaguing my thoughts, this isn't a good thing at all. My heart is seriously broken, today has not been a good day at all, I just want to climb in my bed and shut myself away from the world.

"Let's get you home" He stood up, his arms pulling me up, wrapping around hugging me, fighting back tears, I try to push the thoughts from my mind, thoughts I never want to see again. The drive back we sit quietly, I feel like I have told him my darkest secret. Yet, I didn't even tell him the whole story. Not even Liam knows, and it is not something I tell anyone, I am scared he is just being nice, so it doesn't hurt my feelings, then he will walk away. Walking through the door, Georgina runs to me and hugs me.

"Alena, I was freaking out here, you should have known we would have been worried" I feel sorry for her, I know how much she must have been scared for me I just totally forgot.

"She's okay, no harm done. She just needed some space" Jackson explaining to her why I was hiding, she seemed to glare at him, Liam looks at us confused, he seriously has no idea what is going on or why people would be worried over me staying out for a few hours.

"Oh, I get it you finally told her and now she's freaking out your ex is coming back to get her" Liam's assumption making Georgina look confused, shaking my head at her to just leave it.

"Look, I need to go to bed, I'm worn out, I will see you all tomorrow" Walking off, not saying goodbye to Jackson, I climbed into bed, tears beginning to fall and not stopping as I fell asleep. Waking up, my eyes looking around the room, my mouth is dry from the alcohol, I don't even know what time it is, walking towards the door, I opened it hearing Georgina's voice, peeking through she sat with Jackson both with a drink in their hands.

"You do realise she's broken, don't you? Max made sure of that before she got away from him. She got used to having no freedom, not having a say in where she could go. She didn't even see her family for over a year, she showed up at my house, black and blue covered in blood, that was the last time she saw him" Flinching at her words, I purposely left that part out, Jackson's fist clenching, his whole body shaking with anger, he looks about ready to kill someone.

"Didn't she tell you all of this? Please don't tell her I said anything, I have put my foot in it now. She will kill me if she finds out" Georgina realising she messed up.

"Max sounds like a right piece of work, where is he now?" Jackson asked, looking at her.

"No idea, she changed universities, moved half way across the country, I came with her, he got out a year ago, she was an absolute mess" Sitting on the floor next to the door I listened to them.

"What sort of man would hit a woman and lock her away?" He shook his head, like the whole thought was crazy.

"He did more than that, I don't know how much she told you but, he did a lot more" Her head fell, looking at her his eyes widened.

"Are you saying he, you know" He couldn't bring himself to say it, she just nodded.

"Look, you're the first guy since Max, something made her snap out of being safe, made her go out after university alone, in a way that is a good thing, your good for her, I think, the fact she stood up to you and Liam yesterday was amazing, she has not stood up for herself or spoke up in years" He nodded looking at her.

"Just don't fuck her over, as I said she is broken, there is no guarantee she will make another relationship like that. I am amazed she spoke to you, honestly, she hasn't even told me the full extent, she was alone with the case worker when she told her everything, me I got a few short sentences she never tells anyone" He nodded to her.

"I was thinking that, maybe I am not right for her, somethings in my life I don't know if she can cope or handle it, but I like her, I don't know why, but in a way she has already helped me, I have not been with anyone since Caroline. To be honest, I would give everything up to keep her if she didn't like it. What is Max's last name?" I hope she doesn't say. Turning so my back is against the wall, I pull my legs up, hugging them listening to Georgina and Jackson talking, slowly falling asleep next to the door. Waking up to the sun shining through the window, I have no idea what time it is, feeling glad I don't have university though. Rolling over I screamed, jumping back, Jackson sat next to me, looking at me confused.

"Good morning beautiful" He is smiling, he seems in a good mood despite what Georgina had told him, the fact I lied to him and he found out. I feel awful, my head hurts, my eyes feel heavy like I have huge bags under them, I know I will look disgusting.

"I highly doubt I look beautiful" I sit up, looking

around the room. How did I get in bed, I fell asleep at the door?

"You do to me, I'll just go grab you a coffee now you're awake" He got up walking out, using this as a chance I got out of bed quickly walking to the bathroom, looking in the mirror, I am shocked I look awful, my eyes are red and puffy from crying, my hair sticking up everywhere, turning the shower on, stepping in the water numbing my body and mind, it feels free everything running away as my body relaxes the feeling amazing, closing my eyes, tipping my head back I let go, everything being washed away. All my worries almost gone, disappearing down the drain with the water, I feel so much better now, getting out I wrap a towel around my body. Walking into my bedroom, jumping I nearly scream. Jackson sat on my bed, holding a coffee, I forgot about him still being here.

"What is it with me scaring you? Do I look like a monster or something?" He laughs, touching his face to make sure it felt okay.

"Have you looked in the mirror lately? You're far from monstrous, I just forgot you were here, that's all" Explaining I climb onto the bed next to him, realising I am wearing just a towel holding it closed tightly.

"You look much better, I am guessing you needed that sleep?" His hand rubbed my arm, his eyes watching me.

"I certainly did, I'm glad I don't have university what

time is it anyway?" I have not even checked.

"It's one thirty, you missed breakfast and dinner" His smile growing.

"Oh, crap I should get up, I have work today. Did you stay over?" My mind trying to remember what happened after I fell asleep at the door, but it was useless.

"I slept on the sofa, I was up late with Liam and Georgina. Georgina was kind, even offered your bed for me to sleep in, Liam however, said I had to sleep on the sofa and kept checking me" He started laughing I can see Liam doing that.

"Yep, that sounds like them two, alright. They never agree on anything" I can't help but laugh along with him. Finishing my coffee, I was moving to get up, his hands pushing me back down, his legs either side of me, my heart feels like It is about to explode through my chest.

"Do you trust me?" His eyes looking into mine, he is clearly talking about what Georgina mentioned last night, is he going to be asking me this every time he goes to touch me?

"Well, you're currently straddling me in my bed, while I wear nothing but a towel, what do you think? My answer is playful, feeling a bit of myself coming back. His lips, pushing down on mine, kissing me fast and violently, his hand grabbing both of my wrists, pinning them above my head as he kissed down my neck.

"I've been waiting for hours to wake you up, I told

myself to behave, but seeing you with just a towel on, I can't control myself" He breaths against my ear, his lips starting to kiss me again, slowly down my neck, taunting me, making me want more. His mouth moving down across my collarbone, down the centre of my chest. His other hand removing the towel from around me, his lips sliding over my nipples, slowly sucking one into his mouth before gently nibbling it, making me moan out loud. Hearing a knock at the front door, I don't want him to stop, his mouth was, so provoking it made me need more.

"Oh, hi, Mrs. Parker, what a nice surprise" My body freezing hearing Georgina's voice. Jackson stops, his eyes quickly looking at me.

"Oh crap, my step mum is here" My hands pushing against his chest, his body unmoving, failing miserably Jackson starts to laugh at my feeble attempt to escape. He began moving, his body lying next to mine, now I am able to move, I get out the bed grabbing the dressing gown and putting it on.

"You should probably stay hidden, unless you want to climb out the window and come back in through the front door" I turned starting to leave, him walking out my bedroom would cause a whole load of questions I don't need or want.

"Alena are you okay?" My step mum walking over to me, her arms wrapping around me.

"Yes, why wouldn't I be?" I look at her, confused.

"Georgina sent a text yesterday to your dad saying

71

you had gone missing, she kept us updated, we knew you were found, but I still felt like I should come check you were okay myself, especially after everything that has happened lately" Her arms wrapping around me tighter.

"Thanks Georgina" I muttered under my breath.

"Wait, what do you mean after everything that has happened lately" She is looking at me like I am confused.

"Didn't your dad tell you? Max showed up at our house a couple of times a few weeks ago, he keeps coming back to check you're not with us" Her words are making me feel dizzy and sick, I need to sit down, I feel weak stumbling I hear Georgina calling my name. Waking up, I feel distorted and confused, Georgina, Jackson, Liam and my step mum all looking down at me, I passed out, didn't I? I want the floor to swallow me up, everyone is looking at me concerned, it is embarrassing.

"Are you okay Alena? What happened, I heard Georgina shout your name I came running through to see you on the floor, somebody tell me what's going on" Liam sounds pissed off.

"Liam shut up. Not everything is about you" Jackson pointed out.

"And who are you exactly? Why did you come out of my daughter's room?" My step mum looking at Jackson, she doesn't look pleased with him.

"I am her boyfriend, what made her pass out?" Jackson looks around worried, the word boyfriend making me smile.

"Maybe she passed out from shock after what you told her has been happening Mrs. Parker?" Georgina offered.

"Why, what's been happening" Liam asking again.

"It doesn't matter right now, Darling are you okay, can you hear us?" My step mum kneeling next to me.

"Yes, I can hear you all, I am fine, just lack of sleep and too much booze, you all need to lay off a bit" Getting up I walked to the kitchen, everyone watching me, waiting, grabbing toast I walk back through, Liam goes to his room which I am grateful for. Sitting I talk to my step mum, keeping the conversation off Max and more about university, work and well Jackson, my step mum leaving an hour later, clearly realising there was no need to be here, I promised her I would call and keep her updated on how I am feeling. Heading back to my room, Georgina following me, getting into the room, I turn to face her.

"You told Jackson, didn't you?" I look at her waiting, wondering if she will admit it or not.

"I'm sorry, he said you told him everything, I didn't think, I honestly thought he already knew everything" She shook her head, like she was in trouble.

"It's fine, he knows now so he can leave if he wants to" Why does my mind seem so set on him walking away from me?

"Don't be daft Alena, for some strange reason, he's very attached to you. You both seem to be drawn to each other, like magnets. How do you feel about Max, are you going to tell Jackson?" She looks at me questioning.

"I don't really know how I feel, I guessed he would go to their house at some point, but I didn't think he would keep an eye on the house in case I returned. I'm really scared he might have followed her here" The fact she came here knowing that he has been watching the house could mean he knows where I am now.

"You have to tell Jackson everything, he might be able to protect you in ways me and Liam can't, think about it Alena, do the right thing" Shaking my head I disagree.

"Thing is Georgina, I don't want him to know, I know it sounds crazy, but I don't want him to be on guard and asking for permission before touching me, I could tell this morning you told him, adding this on so early on he won't even want to hold my hand for fear I will freak" My head lowering the door swinging open.

"You don't need to tell me anything, because I heard everything. Weren't you aware that you two were shouting at each other? Even Liam heard, and now wants to know everything" He looks at me like he is shocked I wouldn't tell him, this is just one big mess, it would be so much easier if I had not met Jackson, somehow him in my life complicates things so much more.

"You're coming to my house, I mean it, you're not safe here, so you're staying with me" He was insistent.

"No chance, she hardly even knows you, she will be safe here, she has me and Georgina to protect her" Liam argues back, this is like the other night all over again. Jackson turning to Liam his laugh menacing.

"So, you think you can look after her and protect her, do you? You'll know what to do if a man you don't even know grabs her? How are you going to stand up to a man when you're just a boy Liam?" Jackson spat back.

"Enough, this is just like the other night, you two are just making things worse. Liam, you need to accept that Jackson is the one she wants, and Jackson you need to stop purposely winding Liam up! Look, we don't know for certain that he followed her, if he didn't follow her then she'll be living in your house for no reason" Georgina now trying to reason with them both, they are all talking about me like I am a child, like I can't speak for myself, I hate when people do this.

"Guys, I'm okay here for now, Jackson I promise we will call you if anything happens, I'm not leaving my life here for something that might never happen" I hope explaining it like that makes them see sense.

"Okay, well, I need to go. I have work to do if anything happens, call me straight away" Jackson kissed me before walking out, Georgina and Liam leaving the room, climbing in bed, I lay down, the past few days have been awful, how can two people getting together cause so much drama so quickly? Yet at the same time it has been wonderful, and I doubt I would change it even if I had a choice, I have no idea what is going to happen next, all I can do is wait and see. Waking up, dazed, I try finding the button for my alarm to turn it off, hitting it the room fell silent, finally back to normal. Walking into the shower, I can't wait for today, I can't wait to see Jackson and just enjoy the rest of my time with him. Getting dried and dressed, I walk into the kitchen Georgina sat quietly, joining her for breakfast I sat waiting.

"You do realise I've not forgotten right? I want all the details when we get a chance, maybe a girl's night out?" A laugh of disbelief escaping my lips, hearing her night out thoughts.

"A girl's night out, do you not realise that all of these events happened because of your last night out that you planned?" I am joking, but there is no way I am doing another night out.

"Okay, fine, what about a girl's night in? We'll send Liam away for the whole night. It'll just be us two, on the sofa, chick flicks and wine. What do you say?" She looks so hopeful how can I say no, to be honest a night in sounds great. Just us two, I need to talk and let off steam without anyone else being able to hear.

"Why not, I could do with a girl's night in" My body

relaxing a little realising that I wouldn't be dragged out.

"I will walk with you, I have got class this morning as well" Georgina grabbed her coat walking towards the door.

"Okay, great, where's Liam?" I looked around realising I haven't seen him, maybe she has.

"He left before, no idea where he went though, I am guessing he is just avoiding the awkwardness of last night" Georgina explained as we walk out of the apartment. It feels good to be back to normal, walking to university, we spent a lot of time laughing and talking like we usually do.

"Have you noticed, Liam is completely fine when getting up and going out, but he struggles to make a cup of tea or even scratch his own leg?" Georgina laughed, nodding I have to agree.

"He is definitely milking it, it's probably because he lives with two women, he is expecting us to act like nurses" Joking with her, Liam is one to push boundaries. I have missed this, who would have thought a few short days everything would change, as much as I like Jackson I do wonder if it is worth it. Maybe we both have too much baggage to make it work? It sounds completely crazy, but I am starting to feel like I love him and I haven't even known him a week. Arriving at university, we planned to meet after our lessons, while she makes out it is just to walk home together, I know it is because she is trying to be protective just in case, I don't blame her though, considering everything we found out last night, had it been the other way around I would be just the same.

"Hey beautiful" Smiling, I recognise the voice without even looking.

"Hey Daz, how are you? You know, you shouldn't be calling me beautiful" I turn to him smiling.

How can I not? It would be rude of me to ignore your beauty" He will never change, he is always flirty but never pushing too hard, I don't want him to change either.

"How's your girlfriend? You keep saying she exists, but I've seen no evidence yet, will she mind you calling me beautiful?" He always claims he has a girlfriend, never does have one, but like to claim he does.

"She is coming in two weeks actually, so it'd be great if you could come and meet up with us for a few drinks" He grinned, wow I am shocked.

"Well, I have to say I am shocked that you actually have a girlfriend I can physically meet, not just mentally. I am having a girl's night in that weekend with Georgina trying to stay out of trouble" Laughing while feeling excited about it.

"You, trouble? I have never known you to get into any trouble" He is now laughing along with me.

"Maybe we could meet up, and she could join you and Georgina? She's new in town and could do with some new friends" His smile clearly hoping I will agree, how can I talk to Georgina with someone else there, who I don't even know? How can I confide in her about Jackson, Max and even Liam when they're so personal to me with someone else there?

"Okay then, I'll come with you on Friday after university, if we get on alright then of course she's welcome to join us" I could do with more friends, and if Daz likes her, she has to be nice.

"You two will get along amazingly, I promise! You'll see what I mean, you'll be like two peas' in a pod" He grinned, clearly happy, as he walked out the hall waving goodbye. Classes were slow, boring and Jackson does not help with his constant text messages asking me if I want to go see him and keep him company. I keep saying no but I really want to go, I am not strong enough to keep refusing, and if he stood in front of me, I know I wouldn't. Classes ending, I begin heading outside, Georgina is standing there waiting for me.

"Are you ready to leave?" She looked at me waiting to start walking home.

"Yes, but sorry to say, I've made plans with Jackson, he's taking me out for food, so I'll see you later?" Giving her a cuddle, I smile, I hope she doesn't think I am abandoning her.

"Hey, it's fine with me, just means more chicken for me without you there, considering Liam doesn't eat chicken on a bone. I'll wait here with you anyway. I'm excited to find out everything at the weekend, when it is just us two, a nice girly night in"

"Three" I say it quietly hoping she won't hear or

that if she does she won't go crazy.

"Three? Why three? Please don't tell me you invited Jackson to a girl's night, that's just ridiculous" She looked at me shaking her head, like I would invite a guy.

"No, of course I haven't. Remember Daz who sort of.... Follows me around university?" I question her wondering if she remembers him.

"You're brining Daz, Alena that is even worse" She shook her head.

"No, not Daz. His girlfriend, he finally has one and she is coming up that weekend and apparently, she's staying a while. I'm meeting her on Friday. I want to invite her round Saturday for a few hours" I can't believe she thought I had invited Daz.

"Fair enough, I'm definitely going to tell her that he fancies you though" She started laughing, typical Georgina always one to ruin someone's happiness with the truth, Jackson pulled up in his car, smiling I climb in.

"I can drive you home if you want Georgina?" He looked at her as I fastened my seat belt.

"Erm... no thank you, three is a crowd and I don't want to sit in a car with you two lovebirds" She laughed walking away.

"So, I think we will go for food first" Jackson started the engine.

"Sounds good to me, you can choose where" Driving there we stayed quiet, pulling up in the restaurant car park, his phone starts ringing, picking it up he answers immediately.

"Hello, Mr. Reeves here" His voice sounds so professional, I am guessing it is business, he sat listening for a few seconds.

"Can't this be resolved without me? It's literally a five-minute job, I'm busy where's Leah?" He doesn't sound happy at all.

"Right, I will be there soon" He hung up the phone turning to face me.

"Sorry babe, I have to go into work, I will drop you off at your apartment and pick you up when I've finished. He started the car, driving out the car park.

"Seriously, why can I just not come with you, are you still keeping your business a secret?" We should know everything as we learnt these things have a habit of biting us when we don't think they can.

"It's not that I want it to be a secret, it depends how open minded you are" He glances over at me, he is being serious.

"Do you deal drugs or something? I think if we both want this relationship to work, then we need to be honest and open with each other, I mean, look at the mess already from us not telling each other things" So much mess, my mind tries to remind me of it all, I need to know what his business is, I don't want six months to past before I find out and realise I don't like it.

"Okay, fine, you can come, but don't say I didn't warn you" He turned to face me smiling, but it is more of a just you wait and see look, that makes me feel nervous now.

"Just promise me one thing, you won't run without asking questions and finding out the truth, you might misinterpret it and I wouldn't want you thinking it is something it isn't. Remember not even Liam knows about it" Nodding in agreement, I sit quiet, after around fifteen minutes, I feel restless, how far are we going?

"Okay, so where are we going, china? Is your business really this far away?" I look at him curiously.

"Yes, well, one of them is anyway, I told you my business is open in a few locations, sometimes it has a few problems and I have to call in. We'll be arriving in around fifteen minutes" the car falling silent again, my mind throwing ideas at me, I need to ask I can't just sit and wait.

"So, it isn't selling drugs?" I need to keep an open mind, if I guess right, I need to not freak out.

"No, that's a bit over the top, don't you think?" He is laughing, at least that's a good sign it means he isn't offended by my guessing wrong.

"Okay, is it weapons?" Prompting him to reply.

"Yes! That's right, I sell guns and grenades for a living" He is laughing more, what he serious? Looking at him, he turned and winked, okay, he was joking, that is good, because honestly guns and weapons is just wrong.

"Look, it isn't illegal. You're way off with your guesses, just keep an open mind and wait and see"

Well the fact it is legal is good, it doesn't help with me guessing what it is though, now the list has just shrunk down to no options at all.

"Fine" Huffing, I sat back, rather annoyed that he wasn't giving any details away at all, sitting my mind thinking what it could be.

"You're a pimp!" I yelled it a bit too loud in triumph to guessing right. He burst out laughing, shaking his head at me.

"You're one of those people that'll keep on guessing and guessing, aren't you?" He looked at me smiling.

"Yes, so just tell me now and save the hassle" Smiling back, I bite my lip, feeling the pull towards him.

"No, I am amazed though, this is not the girl Georgina described to me, the quiet one, who never says much and isn't all that fun" His eyes looking into mine, Georgina has said a lot about me clearly.

"This is a little bit of me, there is a lot hidden away and not playing, you just make me feel comfortable for some reason" He nodded at me smiling.

"Well, that might change after you see this" We pulled into a drive, sitting quiet I watched the building get closer, in the middle of the countryside, maybe I got it wrong and he owns farms or something. As the house got closer I notice it is a mansion, the sign outside saying 'Seductive Vibrations' What have I possibly just agreed to walk into? Jackson looks at me, my face must have said it all, what sort of business is Seductive Vibrations?

"I said this wasn't a good idea, that you probably are not open minded enough. We're not even inside yet and you have a look of pure terror on your face, I will turn around and take you home" He sounds annoyed, I don't blame him. Did I really want to see this, could I really let him take me home without even looking inside? The fact is this could be the last chance I have to find out what it is for a long time, because if I freak out now I doubt he will invite me to look again. The suspense is killing me though, I can't ignore it, I need to know what it is, but this seems to be his biggest secret.

"No, I will come inside, I am fine, honestly, I was just taken aback by the sign, open mind, 100% I won't run if I find it too freaky I will just ask to try ease my thoughts" He turned looking at me, assessing if I was being serious, I am I want to know I don't want there to be secrets and lies between us.

"Okay then, if you're sure" He stopped the car, getting out we walked up the steps towards the entrance, it was beautiful inside, breathtakingly amazing.

"Mr. Reeves, how lovely it is to see you" A woman approached us, she was dressed in a black dress holding a tray full of drinks.

"Hello Anna, where is Samantha?" He looked around seeming trying to find the woman in question.

"She's in one of the staff quarters. She was rather distressed over what happened, but she seems to have calmed down a bit. She's afraid she'll be asked to leave" Jackson looked at her like that was a crazy thought.

"It wasn't her fault. This goes much higher than her, to Leah, who's meant to check everyone before giving out the address" He turned to me, smiling, his hand trailing along my jaw.

"You might want to stay here, Alena" Anna now finally acknowledged me, with a bit of an evil glare.

"No, I'm happy to come" I don't want to stay here with Anna, clearly, she does not like me, or like the idea of Jackson touching me, Jackson wrapped his arm around me, pulling me to his side.

"Are you sure? Once upstairs you might not like what you see, I will tell you again, totally legal, but you might not want to see me again" Anna seemed to smile at that point, clearly, she likes Jackson, but I am guessing he is not the type to date someone he employs.

"Please stop trying to warn me off, I am coming up there with you" He nodded, holding my hand we started walking upstairs, it looks wonderful, how can he be so against me seeing this? Reaching the top of the stairs there is a door saying 'Couple' I can't help but wonder what it is for? We walked through a different door, but lost in my thoughts I didn't notice what the sign said, the hall was dark, there is music playing in the background. A long corridor that seems to have windows on one side. Jackson gripped my hands tighter, looking at me.

"Last chance to turn back Alena" He seriously looks worried, what is ahead? My heart is racing already at the thought, but I can't say no now, nodding I started walking.

Getting to the first window my eyes glance inside, my heart stops for a second not what I was expecting not at all, I felt like running away but at the same time I am intrigued to know more. This business is in a way telling me there is a side of him I don't know about, sure there was a slight hint when we fucked, but this is way bigger than that. The two women inside, one strapped to a bed, the other woman is holding a whip, looking away I don't need to see more. The second window just like the first, however a woman naked, kneeling down with her arms bound behind her back, there was a man and a woman with her. Okay, I can cope with that, my mind is processing the thoughts really well considering, reaching the third window, I feel brave glancing inside. The room dark, but you can clearly see a man and woman having sex, with women and men around watching, playing with themselves. I feel Jackson's pull on my hand, I can feel I am frozen from the shock, shaking it off I begin walking again, this time too fast, Jackson pulling me back to him.

"I know it's not easy, I really believed you when you said you were open minded enough" His mutter quiet as we walked into a room with people sitting around drinking coffee.

"Mr. Reeves! It's great to see you, Anna is in her

office Sir" A young man shook Jacksons hand.

"Thank you" Jackson continued to walk through the office, reaching a door at the end he opened it, us both walking in. Clearly his office, it is huge.

"Can you wait here while I go and find Anna and speak to her please? Jackson looked at me, I want to know who Anna is and what has happened, it sounds important, maybe I am nosey, but I feel I need to know.

"I would rather come, if that's okay?" He rolled his eyes at me.

"Fine, I'll ask someone to fetch her and she can come to my office instead" He opened the office door.

"Can someone get Anna to come to my office, please" He called out and a few people jumped up to get her, closing the door he turned facing me. Standing here in silence shock begins to overtake me, what have I seen, and did I guess right is he some sort of pimp, or maybe a posh brothel? My thoughts are dangerous, I need to remember what I said, open mind and I would ask questions, moving I sit on the chair, my heart rate quickening, a small quiet knock at the door.

"Come in" Jackson called looking at me concerned, the woman walked in, clearly distressed and in tears, I feel sorry for her and I don't even know what has happened, she started talking quickly trying to explain.

"I'm so sorry, it is entirely my fault, I shouldn't have

let her in" Jackson shook his head trying to stop her. "Anna, this is not your fault, this is Leah's fault her job is fairly simple, complete background checks on everyone who books in. She only has to make sure they are who they say they are, that they also don't conflict with other people" He was trying to reassure her.

"She wasn't happy at all Sir, Mr. Spencer also wasn't happy that his wife turned up while he was here. She threatened to sue the company and myself, although I wasn't anywhere near Mr. Spencer, I just checked her in" This is all confusing me totally confusing.

"Anna, you need to remember that he was here for his own reasons, as was his wife. If they keep this part of their lives secret, then that's entirely on them if their partner finds out. Yes, Leah may have made a mistake and booked them in on the same day, but ultimately, if there in a relationship they should have told each other. No relationship can last built on lies, secrets and no communication" He glanced towards me at the end, clearly aiming that part at me as well.

"Take the rest of the week off, get yourself sorted, you will still be paid, I am sorry the customers were rude to you, I will contact them both myself" She nodded, seeming to calm down more.

"Thank you, Sir, I will do" She walked out, Jackson follows her to the door, locking it behind him, sitting on a chair next to me he looks at me.

"So, tell me what you're thinking? Your face looks like you don't even know how you feel at the moment" His voice soft and gentle. Why can all I think about is climbing onto his lap, the thought strong in my mind, the door is locked, no one can come in. Standing up, I walk to him, climbing on his lap, my legs either side of him, his hands gripping my arse, my lips, pushing against his, kissing him, my hands running along his neck, fingers tangling in his hair, moaning the memories of the kitchen flooding my mind, this is not me at all, how has he so easily unlocked me? His hands gripping my arse tight, pulling me to him, moaning my hands slide down, my fingers unfastening his buttons. His hands grabbing mine, looking at him, his eyes delving into mine.

"Again, tell me what you're thinking, other than trying to fuck me in the office, honest thoughts Alena please, otherwise I stop all this right now" His hand swung, slapping my arse, moaning I lean forward, going to kiss him, his head turning.

"Answer" He's looking at me like I am crazy, huffing I sit up on him.

"Okay, so I was right, you're some sort of pimp, you prostitute women out" Maybe that was too blunt, but it is the truth, I should be running why am I not running.

"No, you have it all wrong. It's not like that at all, in the BDSM world, it is known as a dungeon" My eyes widened, what the hell it doesn't look like a dungeon.

"Okay, let me try explain another way. When you were a child, you had fantasies about flying to the moon, walking on it, being a racing car driver all those crazy things right?" He looks at me, I nod, agreeing yes, mine changed so frequently, so I get that bit, but what does that have to do with this place?

"There are places for children to act out their dreams, they dress up as an astronaut, a racer and whatever else. Well, this place is similar but for adults. No money is exchanged here. People can make donations to keep it open, but I don't charge anyone except for food and drinks" His explanation makes sense but still does not make sense either.

"Everyone who works here, tends to clean and look after the guests, things like that. Everyone else are just guests that come to fulfill their fantasies" He is looking at me, I have so many questions.

"Ask away, I can tell you have plenty of questions Alena" Nodding, I find the first one to start.

"These women are not prostitutes, then?" I honestly thought they were.

"No, the women are not paid, it's not just women, there are plenty of men here too" Okay that is good and eases my mind a bit.

"Okay, you say fantasies, what sort of fantasies?" He laughed at my question, I am being serious.

"Sexual fantasies of course Alena, fetishes, all those things, surely you have a sexual fantasy" My face is getting red, I do, but there is no way I am talking about it.

"Okay, so why do these people come here if they have partners? Why do they not do their fantasies with their partners, I still don't know what sort of fantasies people come here for though" Okay, that was a lot more than one question, but I can't stop I have so many.

"Walk with me? If I show you then it'll help me explain better, and you will get a picture of what it is really like" His eyes looking at me, waiting for me to move off him so we can go. Standing up, he grabbed my hand, walking back to the corridor with the windows, he stopped outside the first window, looking inside.

"The people in here are not a couple, they are two people who both have the same fantasy of having sex with others watching them. The man and woman understand that they can leave whenever they like. The windows are here so we can make sure nothing bad is happening without consent, there is a lot of forms and consent to give before going into the rooms" Okay, that honestly now it is explained does not sound or look as scary as before, we moved onto the next window.

"Some women need a submissive in their lives, this is one way how they can get it, if they have people living with them, if they have a partner or don't have room for a playroom, then this is a good alternative" I know a little about Submissive, the whole thing was interesting, I remember Max talking about how he used to have a submissive before me. He turned though, he then pointed out how a Submissive was better than me, how they wouldn't defy him like I did. Jackson was staring at me, clearly realising I was thinking, the look on my face has him asking questions of his own.

"What are you thinking, do you still think I am a pimp? He laughed, but clearly my face was showing worry, not at this just thinking about Max, looking again, the people looked relaxed, happy, it is like they really do want to be in there.

"Okay, you're not a pimp, but how do you earn money from this, do people really make donations?" It seems crazy someone would be willing hand over money if there was no need.

"Yes, you wouldn't believe how many men and women give us donations. Think about it, if we were to close, they would not have a safe place to go to have their fantasy fulfilled. Some people give donations for their partners to come here, they are in a relationship where they know they can't give them their fantasy and are willing to let them come here for it, some relationships are that secure, strong and open that the women can come here and the guy is happy at home while she is" That is crazy, but I guess if you're in a relationship and don't feel you can please someone you would let them, I know I would. Looking back at the room, there is so much in them whips, some bigger than me, chains, bolts, handcuffs, a lot of stuff I also don't know.

"Right, come with me this way" He starts to walk out the room, at the top of the stairs we walked through the door that says 'Couples' on it.

"This side is for swingers, which I am sure you have heard of, some couples come here together with another couple, some couples come with a female to fuck while their partner watched" He is so blunt, the whole thing while it is scary is interesting, and clearly safe, walking down he was right, there were three couples in one room.

"Are they with their partners?" I am shocked, staring at them.

"I don't know, a lot of the time we switch partners, some don't but some do. Look around Alena, people want to be here, there are not forced. Every now and again we get accidents where a husband and wife are booked on the same day" Nodding, we walked forward, my eyes glancing in the room, stopping I watch, a woman on the floor, men surrounding her, a lot of men, she is the only woman in this room, she's smiling, blindfolded and has a collar on, the men are playing with her, one man is sat watching. I didn't realise I was standing for so long.

"You don't seem fazed by this, you were by the couple having sex, yet this room you don't seem to be shocked by seeing it at all" Jackson stood behind me, his arms wrapping around me, I stay looking at her I can't help but smile.

"Something you want to say? A fantasy, maybe Alena?" His mouth next to my ear, shaking my head, I turn facing him.

"No" A smile on my face, I am so bad at lying, but he doesn't seem to be pushing.

"One more question, is this what you do? Do you use this place and are you into everything here?" I look at him, his eyes assessing whether or not to answer.

"Let's go sit down, eat and talk" Walking back out, we walk downstairs, into a small quiet restaurant in the building.

"Mr. Reeves, are you here for a business meeting?" The young waiter enquired.

"No thank you, this one is for pleasure, but still somewhere private to sit" We were led to a small sofa and table, surrounded by drapes. He handed us two menus and walked away.

"Right, so I have used this place for myself, that was before Caroline, though" I nod, wondering if he was going to carry on or just leave it at that.

"I didn't use this place because I can't do these things at home, I used it if there was someone who felt safer been here, then, at my house" He looks at me, assessing me, making sure he is safe to keep going.

"Before Caroline, I was a different person, I met Caroline, she fell pregnant, everything changed, I put the whole world behind me, other than business. I stopped with being a Dominant and Sadist and became normal" Words I know all too well, I feel for him, the fact he gave up a bit part of who he is for Caroline.

"I don't think I could be a submissive, I doubt I would be good at being a submissive for you" I have to be honest, I won't be even Max pointed out that I wouldn't be, how is it I found someone else who is into this?

"Alena, I don't want you to be, I said I put that life behind me, sure it would be nice, but I like you, I am willing to sacrifice it for you. Why would you think you wouldn't be a good submissive anyway" He looks at me waiting, I should just tell him.

"Before me, Max had a submissive" I didn't miss him flinch at the name Max, clearly on edge about it.

"He told me I would be no good as a submissive, because I always defy him, that his submissive did as they were told, and he was pleased in the right ways" The night he told me, clear as anything in my mind, Jackson shakes his head looking shocked.

"Alena, I highly doubt Max was a real Dominant, a real Dominant would not do to you what he did, under any circumstances, so there is your answer, he wouldn't know if you would or would not be good at it, he likes controlling and possibly tried pretending he was a Dominant to use that as an excuse. As I said, I don't expect any of that from you, I am happy just to have you" That upsets me, I don't know why but it does.

"I would like to try, before things got bad, I enjoyed that part, sure it was not full submission, and there is far more in this world, I don't know about, but I would like to try" He's shaking his head, the waiter comes back with our food, setting it down, I began eating, okay I will leave that for another day.

"So, this is just a normal restaurant, or not?" Looking around it looks normal.

"Yes, this is just a restaurant, however, some couples hire quieter tables so that all eyes are not on them, some couples enjoy feeding each other" The thought of feeding someone does not compel to me at all.

"So how many of these do you have?" He said he has a few open before.

"I have quite a few, located all over, really. I have a question for you, would you ever act out your fantasies?" My face is red, instantly red at his question.

"Honestly, I doubt it, I am too shy" He nodded, clearly wanting to ask me what my fantasies where.

"Look, this place is not bad, far from it, it is a safe place. Imagine you wanted to act out your fantasy, this place is an option, it is safe, a lot safer than walking into a bar and going home with 5 blokes and hoping they will stop when you ask. Would you rather come here or look elsewhere to fulfil your fantasy?" Honestly, I am over the shock, the place seems fine, at first, yes, it was scary but now the shock has settled I am fine.

"It is safe, I can see that, I would honestly prefer to come here, then just find random people to do it with" I would, I can see myself here using the place, which is so crazy.

"Are you staying tonight, Sir?" A member of staff came over looking at us.

"No, not tonight I'm afraid" Jackson replied, as we walked towards the exit, getting outside I turn to look at him.

"What did he mean by staying?" Looking at him for answer, do people actually sleep in those rooms?

"I have my own room, bathroom, kitchen and belongings here. It's like a hotel room, it's for when I know I'm needed here" He is stood watching my reaction.

"If you want, we can go back inside, I will show you it is your choice" His offer was perfect.

"Yes, I would like that" he looked at me shocked, I am guessing he thought I was ready to run away from the place and him, his arms pulling me to him, kissing me passionately, leading us both inside we went upstairs, arriving at a door he unlocked it leading my inside. As we stepped through it, his body pinned me against the wall, his kiss forceful, my head spinning, I am pulling him closer to me, wanting to taste him. My fingers clumsily trying to unbutton his trousers, moans escaping my mouth, his hands grasping mine, pinning them above my head, that just makes me so much worse.

"You're so keen, so teasing. I'm here trying to

behave, but you kitten, are making me lose my mind" His words, making me want more, fuck I love him calling my kitten, my hands struggling against his grip, if I can escape I can continue undressing him. It is useless, no success at all.

"You're so calm, but then for some reason when I am near you, you explode like a bomb trying to rip my clothes off" His mouth kissing my ear, his teeth gently biting down, moaning I push my body towards him wanting more.

"All I wanted was a kiss, then you go crazy and try strip my clothes off. You didn't even give me a chance to close the door" He was teasing me, his mouth kissing down my neck, I am going crazy, I need him, trying to behave I stop struggling, my mind freeing itself of all the thoughts as his mouth teased me. Stepping back, he let go of me. My arms pulling him back, the buttons on the shirt falling off as I pulled it, my hands unfastening his trousers, he is he stood there just staring at me, fuck me!

"I won't apologise, in fact, you should. I'm only this crazy because of you. You're the one who's bringing back a side of me, I lost, actually a side of me, I never knew existed" I don't know who this person is, but I love her, I seem to have found myself but also extra parts I never knew existed. Kicking the door closed, I pull him towards me, stumbling back, we both fall in a heap on the floor.

"See what I mean, you're crazy, now you're trying to

kill us both!" My lips push against his, I have had enough of his talking, his arms wrapping around me, pulling me to him, moaning my hands stroke up his chest. He pushes me up shaking his head.

"Can you at least wait until we get to my room" Looking at him confused, he is laughing, gently kissing me on the lips.

"This isn't your room?" I just shut the door that he unlocked so it has to be.

"No, Alena, look around you. It's a corridor, my room is the door near the end" Looking around, he was right, now I feel like a fool, what if someone had seen? Getting up, I feel crazy, I am so intoxicated by him, I can't even think straight. To be honest, I don't care that this wasn't his room, I still want him right here right now. This is all so wrong, so very wrong, how could I be happy with this? He is driving me crazy and making me do things I would never do. Walking into his room, I have a feeling tonight is changing everything for me, changing everything I thought I liked.

3 HEATING UP

Closing the door, Jackson turned, his eyes on mine, grabbing my phone, I quickly tell Georgina I won't be home tonight and not to worry. Now we are in here I feel like I have calmed down, my rationality has come back, and my crazy side seems to have shied away again He began. Lifting me up his body pushing me against the wall, moans escaping my lips, my legs wrapping around him. My hands ripping at his shirt, buttons falling to the floor, my crazy side coming out again.

"Alena, please, can you try to leave at least one button intact?" His voice seductive.

"Well, I could try, but it'd be more fun to just rip them all off" Trying to rip his shirt open, his hand grabbing mine, holding them above my head.

"Do you trust me Alena?" His eyes looking into mine.

"Yes, I do" I begin kissing him again, his mouth on mine, his shaft pushing against me.

"I want to try something, open mind, okay?" Nodding, I agree, his body pushing against mine again, his arms wrapping around me, carrying me to the bed, his mouth kisses me. My hands began to try to rip his shirt open again, he sighs, His hand wrapping something around one of my wrists, holding my hand above my head, then doing the same to the other. Both my hands up high, unable to move, his mouth kissing my body, moaning I push my breasts up towards him, wanting to feel his mouth on them. His lips kissing gently over my breasts, gently sucking into his mouth, his teeth biting down, moaning.

"Now you have no choice but to behave" He chuckled, his kissing teasing me more. I feel my body and mind relax, his mouth continuing kissing down my body. His body climbing onto it, moaning I want to pull him towards me.

"Your top seems to be in the way, and since your hands are stuck I can't take it off, maybe I should rip it off like you did to mine?" His mouth lowered kissing around my top.

"You wouldn't be" I was too late, his hands gripped my top ripping it open, exposing my bare stomach and breasts, stopping my words, my breathing somehow slowing down, at the feel of him taking control.

"Perfect, his lips begin kissing me again, his tongue

teasing every inch of me, he was kissing parts of me that made me want to scream from pleasure.

"Your body is perfect" His mutter quiet as he kept kissing me, his tongue teasing my breasts, licking around the nipple.

"If you want to try, I will let you try, I would rather first see how you react to being tied up and bound, blindfolds before I agree though" Nodding in agreement, I watch as his hand slides the blindfold over, my body relaxing, my mind feeling free.

"You know, a lot of pleasure comes from anticipation, from the mind, from words, not from touching the body. Not knowing what will happen next drives some people crazy" His lips starting to kiss again, meaning I feel him move off the bed, the sound of his clothes hitting the floor, climbing back onto the bed, his mouth begins kissing again, teasing, his hand exploring my body, his mouth teasing, I can feel the wetness between my legs and he has not even touched me there yet. The feel of the toy sliding inside my pussy. His lips starting to kiss my breasts, his tongue teasing my nipples, every movement was like an electricity shooting through my veins, making me feel on fire, the anticipation making me wild, the darkness, unable to see making everything more intense, like the sense of touch has become stronger. His mouth kissing down my stomach, across my hips, my body jumping, the warm liquid being poured onto my hips making me squirm, his tongue trailing along from the outside of my hip to the inside of my legs, licking up whatever he had poured. The feel of the liquid on the other side, making me jump, his tongue again trialing along licking it. Moaning, I wish I could grab and hold him right now, to be able to pull him closer to me.

"What do you want Alena? Do you want me to continue? His voice quiet, his mouth kissing me again.

"Yes please" Panting, I arch my back, pushing my pussy up, begging him to continue. The feather rubbing against my skin, over my breasts, sending shivers down my spine. His mouth kissing down, his tongue trailing over my clit, moaning pushing my hips up to him, the sensations together are driving me insane.

"I want to know your fantasy" His mouth, stopping kissing my clit, his hand stopped with the feather. What?" Is he being serious?

"I want to know your fantasy kitten" His growl melting me, he began to lick and kiss my clit, the feel of leather now running across my breasts, the pleasure is unbearable, I can't see what is coming next.

"Go on, tell me your fantasy" He asks again, the toy being pulled out my sex, something cold being pushed inside to replace it. Moaning, I throw up hips up.

"Not saying" I can hardly breath, his mouth lifting from my body, he has stopped touching me.

"Well, maybe this is where I stop, tell me and I will continue" Is he being serious, he has me right on the edge and now he's not going to let me climax.

"Please Jackson, please carry on" I am begging, I don't care I need just a little more to push me over the edge. Will he really stop and leave it if I don't? I don't feel he will, yet I don't want to risk him stopping.

"You want me to keep going, if so you know what to do" His words teasing, his lips gently kissing between each word.

"Fine, I love this. But I would rather be where you are, and have another woman lying on the bed not me" My face is turning red I know it, I don't have time to think, his hand pushing the toy inside me fast again, the feel of it now vibrating, moaning loud, I wish I could move my hands, with ever tease every moan I keep drawing my legs up until they are nearly wrapped around him. He stopped, moving he now wrapped the leather around my ankles, holding them down, lying here now, hands above my head, legs spread wide open unable to close, I can't see a thing. I have no idea what was coming, moaning I jump the feel of the sting across the top of my leg where the whip hit. While it hurts, it is nice, I want more, it feels amazing. He keeps going, making me scream and moan, I can feel myself get wetter and wetter, his whip hitting me on my clit screaming I nearly climaxed. It is driving me insane, he did it again, this time it was a tap not a whip, he was between my legs, his paddling hitting my clit, the vibrations from the toy, sending me wild, his mouth kissing and caressing my breasts, the vibrator beginning to pulse, I am writhing in pleasure, my words escaping my mouth, I can hear myself begging for his cock, begging for him. He keeps taunting me, teasing my clit and tugging on my nipples, I can feel it arise in my body. My back arching as I feel my juices flowing out, moaning louder and louder, the pleasure becoming unbearable, the tapping is becoming harder on my clit, screaming my body going stiff, then the orgasm taking control, pleasure rippling through my body, shaking from it I have never felt anything like it before, his hand pulled the toy out quickly. He moved quickly, his hands unfastening me, pulling me up, kneeling on the bed, his cock pushing against my mouth, opening I begin slowly sucking his cock into my mouth, moaning feeling the hardness, his hands tying mine behind my back. Moaning the sharp sting across my butt from his hand, making me jump, growing wetter, sucking his cock harder, one of his hands grasping my hair, holding my head in place as his hips move, his other hand rubbing my butt, then gently smacking it, sending me wild. My moans getting louder, his hand pulling my hair, my head moving back as his cock falls out my mouth, the coldness of something clipping onto my nipples. His hands grasping my waist, throwing me down onto the bed, his hands tying mine above my head again, pulling me to him, my ass in the air, his cock pushing against my sex, my hips pushing down on it, moaning feeling the length of him inside me. His thrusts became harder and faster, the metal on the nipples beginning to vibrate. His hips moving in rhythm, his hips beginning to move faster, his hand grasping my hair, pulling my head back, my moans getting louder as his other hand grabbing my throat, holding it tight. I love every single part, every sensation, his hips pushed hard and deep inside me, my moans turning to screams, his grip around my neck getting harder, choking me, as he sent me over the edge, my whole body shaking, buckling and giving up. His own pleasure rising, as his hips pound harder and faster into me, moaning as he releases himself, his grip losing on my hair and neck, letting go of me I fall to the bed, moaning exhausted already. His hands untying me, his mouth kissing along my body. The blindfold sliding off, then the clamps from my nipples, his hand lifting the blanket and covering me, too exhausted, I close my eyes sleep taking me, never have I experienced anything like that before, if it weren't for Jackson I'd never have experienced anything like it. Waking up, Jackson is laid next to me, unmoving assuming he is asleep, my hand moved slowly stroking down his chest, I don't think I will ever get enough of him or his love. His hand moves, quickly grasping mine, a smile forming at his mouth.

"Good morning baby" His eyes opening slowly,

looking at me.

"Plan today?" What can be the plan for today? I should be at work and university, but honestly, I would rather spend all my time here with him.

"I should really go to Uni today" Smiling at the should because I know I am not going to.

"Should? Well, if you should maybe I should behave myself today?" Laughing at his reply I kiss his lips.

"Since when do you behave?" My eyes rolling at the thought of Jackson behaving, it is pure craziness. He chuckles, his body moving quickly, pinning me to the bed, his lips kissing across my body, screaming I try to push him away.

"No, stop I mean it, I should go today" His chuckle quiet as his lips keep teasing.

"Should isn't I am, is it Alena, so I am going to be naughty" His lips kissing my body again, moaning I grasp his hair, his eyes looking up to me, pools of darkness I can get lost him, why do I feel he is hiding himself from me?

"I am going to fuck you so good Alena, that you won't want to go to university ever again" His hands gripping my waist, pulling me down to him, screaming with laughter as he does, his lips pushing against mine. The morning went quickly, spending it in bed, him, teasing me, fucking me and showing me, I am glad I didn't go to university today.

"Come on kitten, we need to go back to mine, and probably eat as well" He stands up, grabbing his clothes, smiling back at me, I should move, I should eat, reluctantly, I climb out the bed, I can't stop smiling, my legs feeling weak, my body feeling weak for last night and this morning. Leaving Seductive Vibrations we drive back to his, my mind peaceful for a change, no questions, no worries, arriving at his we walk to the kitchen, he smiles, standing there him cooking I can't believe how lucky I had got. To think I was just going to walk away from him, I am crazy Jackson is hard to explain, he has changed me in a good way, he brought back the old me, I lost but somehow, he makes the bad seem fine, easy to deal with almost. Sitting watching him cook, I know I should contact Georgina and let her know I am fine yet doing it will be like returning to reality. Grabbing my phone, I look, sure enough missed calls from her, and text messages, I don't even need to look to know what they say, something like. Where are you? Are you okay? Alena I am freaking out, answer Alena, Alena hurry up please. Typical Georgina's way of doing things, going to message I send her a quick one, explaining I am fine, at Jacksons and no need to worry if I don't reply for a while.

"Is she freaking out then?" Looking up Jackson is standing there, holding two plates of food.

"No idea, I am not going to read the 54 messages she has left, I just told her I am fine and not to worry" He laughs placing the plate in front of me, sitting eating, we don't say much else, this is the part I hate, the silence, I have no idea what to say and I hate it. I can't do conversations not like most, I struggle with it, yet with Jackson I can sometimes, like now, though, it feels awkward to silent, but my mind cannot force my mouth to speak.

"So, university tomorrow?" He winks at me, I should say yes, but I honestly don't want to. I will catch up no problem, but right now I would rather have a bit of time off and spend it with Jackson.

"No, I don't think so, I rather liked the wake up I got this morning and I doubt I can do that before university" Thinking back to this morning, a smile creeping across my face, how does he do it? How does he make me want to spend so much time with him already?

"Okay, well while I have no issues with us spending the rest of our time in the bedroom, maybe we should go out somewhere, you know see people or something?" Looking at him, I don't know why he would want to do that, it is pure crazy, I would rather spend all the time in his bed.

"Oh, fuck it, what am I talking about like hell are we going anywhere" His body moved, standing up, he grabs me off the chair, his hands lifting me, my legs wrapping around his body. Kissing me, he pushes me back against the wall.

"I plan to fuck you as much as possible before you leave" His voice almost a growl, moaning, nodding at him I bite my lip, what have I got myself into? Carrying me upstairs to the bed, his eyes making me feel safe, yet at the same time, like I am being hunted.

"I am like a wolf Alena, this wolf needs its kitten fix, and you are that kitten" His mouth beginning to kiss me again moaning, I pull him to me, pushing him over.

"This time, I am taking charge" His eyes watching, his hands twitching, he really doesn't do the whole women taking control does he, watching as my hands grasp, his to tie him to the bed, his eyes full of wonder, his hands looking misplaced, they shouldn't be tied to the bed, and he knows it. He doesn't stop me though, he indulges my craziness, slowly kissing along his body, I begin teasing, every inch of him. Time passes and feeling like I have teased him enough, I move, slowly lowering myself on his cock. My hips moving slowly, his control slipping away, I can see it, he hates not being in control, his head shaking, a growl escaping his lips, his hands ripping from the bed breaking the restraints. His hands grasping me, throwing me over.

"Kittens don't take control" His words taking over my body there is no escape for me, I lost all sense of time, I spent it all with him in his bed, two weeks had passed and we had not seen anyone or left his house, passing out I feel exhausted, my body not used to so much sex, pleasure and intimacy, falling asleep I know I will sleep for ages.

Standing in darkness, unable to see anything around me, I can hear screams, I recognise the voice, I just can't figure out who it is, following the screams, I get closer, the figure coming into view, I can see his face, screaming as pain shoots through my head.

Jolting upright in bed, looking around I begin to wonder how I'd gotten here, Of course, I know how I came to be here, I just don't see how my entire life has shifted so drastically in only a few short months. I've been having this dream, or rather nightmare a lot lately, and it proceeds to constantly wake me up. Hoping it wasn't true, I'd normally push it to the rear of my head, attempting to forget it, straining to cover it. The crazy thing is, I am not this type of person at all, He has taken over my life, changed me so much, I don't recognise myself anymore, that is a lie, I see my old self, the old me I lost years ago. I wish to recognise where things are going next, but right now I feel like I'm losing control of my life, I was happily ensconced in my little routine. I'd go to university, then to work, then I'd go home; simple, and uncomplicated. He's turned everything upside down, I can't find my way back and even if I could, I don't think I'd want to. He makes me happy, sitting here on his bed, still somewhat shaken up, I can't conceive of anything else but the same recurring nightmare, is he making me happy enough, or is this simply one big mistake? Hearing the door unfastened, I know instantly it is him without even looking, when he walks into a room, I pick up on it straight away, putting up my head I look towards the door and sure enough, there he is.

"Good morning baby, you look refreshed" I can't help but grin at him, somehow he has defined all odds, made me want to live life again, and love it.

"I guess I have you to thank for that" I say sheepishly, my cheeks flushing pink, even after he's seen me at my most vulnerable, I still feel insecure. I can't help but avert my eyes whenever he calls me baby.

"I thought that maybe today we could have some fun?" His body climbing onto the bed, I begin to laugh.

"No, I don't mean that kind of fun, unless that's what you require? I mean we could just stay in all day and explore each other more..." His body moving closer to me, how is he always in such a good mood? His hands started grabbing my body, I can't help but laugh, I jump back, my hand throwing up telling him to stop.

"No Jackson, I think we can behave for today, I have things that I need to do anyway. I have to go to my apartment as I haven't been back there all week" He pouted looking down at me, my breathing quickening under his gaze.

"Plus, I promised Daz I'd meet up with him and his girlfriend" I've got to admit, I have missed my apartment so much, and it seems like forever since I last saw my friends. We've spent two weeks in his room, hardly leaving. I skipped university, I am guessing I have lost my job as well now.

"Fine, come on babes, let's get you home" Getting

ready, we walked to the car, climbing in he started the engine.

"Hey, can you take me to the centre, I need to grab a few things, I will make my way home from there" Smiling at him, I slightly nudge his arm, as he begins to drive.

"Of course, babes" We sit quietly, after 15 minutes, finally reaching the centre he parks up the shops surrounding us, kissing him I climb out the car.

"Catch you after baby" He smiles, driving off down the street, turning I begin to walk into the shops, shopping was dull, as always, I hate shopping, I detest a lot of girly stuff, just give me a blanket and a chick flick and I am happy. Getting home the flat is quiet, too quiet in fact. It feels so surreal, I haven't been alone for two weeks. Things have changed so much, there is no going back now, there is no way I can go back to being the person I used to be. Appearing about the flat I can't help but smile seeing the kitchen, the kitchen that changed so much in one night, even so I still possess a sense of doom the feeling never leaving no matter what I do.

My phone begins to ring, looking at it, I see Daz's name, my eyes look at the time, I am meant to be there now meeting him.

"Sorry Daz, I'm on my way now, oh, I forgot to ask, what's your girlfriends name?" Grabbing my coat, I leave the apartment.

"You better hurry, she is called Jessica, we're waiting for you" He hung up the phone quickly, me rushing there, how did I forget? Finally reaching the student bar I walk in, seeing Daz, he gets up cuddling me.

"Finally, you're here Alena. Jessica this is Alena, one of my friends, Alena this is Jessica my girlfriend" He introduced us, turning to look at her I freeze for a second, she resembles me, she is short, fiery red hair, and freckles.

"Sorry I'm late, I got distracted" I need to apologise, sitting down I look at her she looks so like me.

"Yeah, I know. You missed university for two weeks, apparently you were too busy with your new fella, Jackson isn't it? Georgina told me" he is teasing me, laughing I nodded.

"Doesn't matter, what I was doing, it's no one's business but mine" Georgina and her big mouth.

"So, Jackson your boyfriend then?" She looks at me smiling, nodding in response to her it feels weird saying I have a boyfriend.

"So how long have you two been together then?" Looking at them, I wait, he always said he had a girlfriend, but always lied so I have no idea.

"About three weeks, around the time you started dating Jackson, we should do a double date sometime" Daz smiling thinking his idea is brilliant, Jessica however, does not like the idea of it at all, the look on her face says it is the worst idea ever.

"Not too sure, Jackson works a lot so might be hard, but I will think about it" I don't want to cause an argument and clearly Jessica hates the idea, sitting we talked for a little while, Jessica seems lovely, so nice and kind. I guess she can come to our girl's night in tomorrow, would be nice to have another friend who is actually nice.

"So, Georgina and I are having a girly night in tomorrow if you want to join us?" Turning to Jessica I smile, she is nice.

"If you can tear yourself away from Jackson that is" Daz quipped.

"Oh, shut it Daz, I would love to come, if that's okay? I don't want you to feel forced into inviting me" Laughing at Jessica shooting Daz down I like her a lot.

"No, of course not, I'd love it if you could come. It'll be a good idea, to get to know each other better if you're going to be spending a lot of time with Daz" I don't want me and Daz to fall out if we don't get along.

"I'm surprised you haven't run away from him yet, I know myself how full on he can be sometimes" I laugh, she looks shocked but then laughs as well, Daz does not look impressed.

"Listen, I've got to go, it was lovely meeting you Jessica, I'll see you tomorrow. Any time after six is fine" She got up, giving me a hug goodbye.

"You smell lovely" She smiled, looking at her confused.

"Sorry, the smell it just reminds me of someone that's all" Her explanation didn't help much, walking out I try to smell my top, but all I can smell is

Jackson, I look back at her and feel slightly uneasy, though why I don't know. Walking back home, my mind is on Jessica, maybe it is just me who is over thinking it all? Walking in Georgina is waiting for me.

"You're back, finally, so was she horrible what happened?" Wow fire away with questions why don't you Georgina.

"Actually, she was really nice, a little weird but nice. She has red hair, slightly taller than me, but looks quite similar" My memory replaying her in my mind, something doesn't feel right.

"He couldn't get the real Alena, so he has gone out and found a fake one? That sounds about right for Daz" She laughed, I have to shake my head, she is going to cause trouble I know it.

"Don't be mean, she did seem nice, you'll find out for yourself tomorrow night" I hope she is nice to her, the last thing I want is Georgina thinking it is funny to say something and Daz finding out.

"How come you said she was weird?" She is looking at me questioningly.

"I'm not sure, I felt like she was constantly assessing me, maybe she thinks Daz likes me? Then when I was leaving she hugged me, and said I smelt nice and reminded her of someone. Plus, she was totally freaked out by the idea of us having a double date" I feel uneasy.

"Well, Jackson does wear nice cologne, it's popular but very expensive. Maybe that's why? You're probably worrying too much to be honest. As for a double date, if she thinks Daz like's you then maybe she doesn't want you two spending so much time together? So, she is definitely coming tomorrow then? I need to know in advance, so I can practice behaving." She seems too pleased that Jessica is coming, so she better behave.

"Yes, she'll be coming any time after six, behave Georgina" I laugh, hopefully she does not mention Daz likes me.

"Right, and is she going to be leaving early or staying over? Because I really want to know how Jackson is in bed, I still haven't found out any details" her elbow nudging me playfully, I can't help but smile and blush.

"You know what, we have time now, so sit down. Just a quick catch up, I've really missed you Alena, this place isn't the same without you" She walked to the sofa sitting waiting for me to follow, I guess I can live with it walking over I sit next to her.

"Okay, what do you want to know? Maybe try one or two questions at a time, not like fifty" Laughing at my expression she knows she does it.

"Where do I start, obviously you've done the deed, so what was he like? What is he hiding? The way he had up on the kitchen counter when we walked in on you was unlike anything I have ever seen before" Wow, straight in with the big questions.

"I'm not sure how best to answer that Georgina, so yes, we've had sex"

"When, how, where and what happened?" She just has to interrupt me, insisting on knowing every fine detail, this is why we need a full night to talk.

"The morning of Liam's accident, we went to the bar, sat talking, then we went back to his house, he kind of fucked me in his kitchen on the side" It sounds weird saying that out loud far too weird.

"You had sex in the kitchen, what is it with you two and kitchens? I want details, clearly you have-not only done it once, when else have you done it?" She is digging, I can't blame her it was Georgina all over, she digs for as much information as she can get.

"We had sex at his work, well kind of. It was his apartment inside his work, business, it's hard to explain, then every day at his house as well" I can't say much about his work, Georgina is not one to understand, and she blabs so Liam would find out quickly as well.

"Okay, so thinking back, what was amazing about it and what did you love?" More questions, she really wants all the details. Remembering back, I feel the smile on my face, him restraining and blindfolding me heighten my pleasure, the image of Max restraining me flew into my mind, the difference is unreal, with Jackson it was love, safe, consensual and enjoyable. With Max it was hate, scary and to stop me running away from him, a tear rolling down my cheek as I remember, how different two men can make the same thing is amazing.

"Did he hurt you, why are you crying, did you force

you? I swear, I will kill him" Georgina now on the warpath ready for blood.

"No! It was perfect, is it weird the thing I hate about Max I love about Jackson?" Looking at her while I ask, her face changed.

"Love? What did you hate about Max that you love about Jackson? You're worrying me now Alena" She is panicking.

"When we used to argue, Max would grab me and restrain me, so I couldn't fight back, sometimes he made me face the wall, so I couldn't see when he was going to hit me, it hurt more when I didn't expect it, everything he did hurt me" I can't go into too much I feel sick thinking about all this, this is hard to explain far too hard.

"Wait, are you saying Jackson did this to you, and you like it? Why would you be with someone that is the same as Max? Alena you need to get out, he is abusing you, and you think it's love, just like you did with Max, you need to leave now!" She is angry, shouting at me, frustrated, she hasn't understood it at all, I need to make her see the difference.

"No! He hasn't hurt me, you're not listening, give me a chance to finish. The time in the kitchen, he laid me on my back, holding my hands above my head, I wasn't scared, I enjoyed it and only during sex" She looked at me trying to work out what I was saying.

"He had me pinned to the side at one point, so I couldn't move. I know if I had said stop he would have, this is going to sound a bit crazy, so don't freak out. He had me blindfolded and chained to the bed" Covering my eyes, I peek through my fingers at her, she looks shocked, she doesn't understand at all.

"Like I said, I knew he would stop, if I said to stop he would. I enjoyed it, it wasn't scary, it didn't hurt me, and it wasn't through hate or anger. I wasn't waiting for a smack or a punch like Max used to, I felt safe, like I could trust him 100%. Ever since I left Max, I felt that a part of me was missing, Maybe it's this? No, I'm not saying I want to be beaten again or forced into doing something I don't like, I mean with Jackson it's different, it's like love" She was still looking confused, how else can I explain it to her, so she understands?

"I'm trying to understand Alena, but it's hard. How can you think it's right after everything you went through with Max?" This is why I wanted to wait till tomorrow night, I knew she would take ages to understand.

"Okay, with Max, I didn't have a choice, he forced me and if I screamed he would grip me tighter and cover my mouth. With Jackson, he makes sure I feel safe, he doesn't hurt me, it's all for pleasure. Max abused me, controlled me, Jackson isn't I have a say and I enjoy it, Jackson isn't doing it out of anger or hate, he's doing it out of love" She looked like she was trying to understand me.

"Right, so it's only during sex? He's not doing it any

other time?" She seems to want reassuring.

"Honestly Georgina, would I look as happy as I do now if he was the same as Max?" Questioning her, she looks at me, smiling as she shook her head.

"No, I haven't seen you this happy in years, so if this kinky stuff if that is what it is, is your thing, then why not" She realises finally, I hope anyway.

"But, I want to know about his business, like right now" She looked at me waiting, if I tell her she would tell Liam, and just like that Liam walked in, I shrug apologetically to her, grateful he was back.

"Who wants food? I brought you ladies some fish and chips" Liam smiled, carrying in the bags of takeaway. Sitting down, we ate, talking and laughing like we usually do, it feels nice, I have missed Liam, he has been avoiding me or, so it would seem, so now is a good time, just like before, before my birthday, before Jackson, before all the mess.

"Alena, I'm happy that you're with Jackson, you look really happy" Liam smiled, that is a shock, I never expected him to accept us that quick.

"Thank you, Liam, I am still sorry for hurting you though, but I am really happy with Jackson" Smiling at him, he smiled back, continuing eating.

"Are you not seeing him tonight?" He looked at me waiting for my answer.

"He's working tonight, so I'm staying here" I wish he wasn't, but I can't keep him to myself all the time.

"Ah, I would have stayed in tonight if I'd have known, I'm going out tonight, unless you girls fancy joining me?" Really, why does everyone want us to go out?

"No thank you, one night out was enough for me, this year, maybe next year" Laughing I winked playfully. I should have an early night, no doubt tomorrow will be a late one, filled with Georgina's questions that even I know I can't escape, I will need sleep for sure to deal with her tomorrow. I have to prepare myself, make sure I sleep because I won't be getting any until well after the sun comes up, lying in bed falling asleep, I feel myself relax. Darkness all around, the man screaming my name, running towards the sound I finally see his face, who is it why can't I make out his face. I should run away, I should because I always get hurt. Something hits me hard, screaming, I jolt awake again, sweating, this nightmare is starting to scare me now, looking at the clock it is only 2am, rolling over I try falling back to sleep, but I can't. Picking up the phone I send Jackson a text.

ME- "I can't sleep! I had an awful nightmare again; this place is too quiet help me fall asleep"

HIM- "Poor Kitten, you could always tell me about your fantasy again, this time in more detail, I would love to know all about it"

ME- "Too complicated to explain"

HIM- "Okay, so you want to be with another woman? So, you're clearly attracted to women then, is there a man involved in your fantasy?"

ME- "Sometimes, yes. But most of the time it's just me and another woman, I can tell it's different being with another woman just from the fantasy, I don't know how I just can"

HIM- "If you ever want to use my business to act out your fantasies, you're free to do so, you know it's 100% safe, I'm happy for you to use my personal room there if you would prefer so no one can see"

Not what I was expecting at all, his reply has totally thrown me, he really wouldn't be bothered if I slept with a woman while in a relationship with him? Lying here considering it would I agree, and could I really do it, the thought of doing it feels amazing yet at the same time I am not sure, I slowly fall asleep forgetting to reply to him.

"Your fantasy can come true if you put your trust in me" The whisper against my ear, making me smile, waking up I look around, I can see Jackson's figure sat on the bed, too tired to move I close my eyes again, glad that he came over falling asleep, I wake back up I keep looking around, catching a glimpse of red in the corner of my eye, there lay a rose, on my bedside table a note beneath it.

"I came by last night, your door was unlocked! I thought I would walk in and see you there, but you weren't so how come the door was unlocked? I won't be around today, I have an issue to sort out, you won't notice I am gone don't worry but I'll be watching you still, back tonight, won't be too late, I can't wait to see you again"

Rolling over I can't help but smile, I have no idea what I will do today, I planned to see Jackson, sure that plan was my plan I had not even asked if he was busy. I lost my job because I spent those two weeks with him, Georgina is out all day at work and no doubt Liam will be sleeping off last night. The day went slow, I was lazy hardly moving off the sofa, checking my phone every minute in case Jackson had text, after four films Georgina finally walks through the home.

"Nibbles, food and alcohol, oh and DVD's although we won't exactly be watching much" She put them down, looking around.

"No Liam?" Shaking my head at her we heard the door, walking over I open it, Jessica stood there smiling.

"Come in Jessica, Georgina this is Jessica, Jessica, this is Georgina" She smiled at Georgina.

"I can see why Daz likes you Jessica" Georgina laughed as she walked in, glaring at her I shake my head mouthing Don't at her. Sitting we spoke about our current partners, Georgina feeling like she was the extra part not having one. Getting up Jessica goes to the toilet, Georgina looking at me.

"She is so like you, seriously it is strange looking at her, you could almost be sisters" Sitting talking after a few hours, we were explaining how we all knew each other, Jessica was explaining she met Daz while back in town, she is trying to track someone down and he offered to help her.

"Whose is this?" Georgina walks out the bathroom holding up a jacket.

"Maybe it's Jackson's? He was here last night, oh

yeah, you left the door unlocked" I accuse her.

"No, I definitely locked it, is that how Jackson got in or did you let him in?" She is looking at me worried.

"No, I woke up, he was next to me on the bed, I was too tired, fell asleep straight away, he left a note though" Getting up I walk to my room grabbing it showing her. She is looking at it confused, she put it on the table and I notice Jessica looking at it weirdly, I won't ask why but it seems a bit suspicious, why would she be keen to see what the note said.

"Was Liam home? Maybe he left it unlocked accidentally if he came back drunk?" I can't remember even hearing Liam.

"I don't think so, I haven't seen him today at all, I assumed he'd be in his bed asleep?" I am starting to worry now, where is Liam?

"No, he texted me at like six, told me he left early" Georgina explains, it helps a bit, at least I know he is safe.

"Well, I guess one of us forgot, let's just forget it and talk about something else" We started to relax, laughing and drinking, Jackson calling me I walk into my bedroom.

"Hello there" I am laughing, trying to stop myself from laughing.

"Okay, you're drunk, aren't you?"

"A little bit, yes, why?" Laughing at his comment.

"Well, I am on my way home, I could come get you if you want to come see me for a bit" Oh, I would love to see him and go there.

"I would love to see your naked body again, but tonight is a girl's night and Georgina will shout at me if I leave" He laughed, clearly realising I was too far gone to save.

"Okay kitten, I will see you tomorrow" hanging up I walk back in, smiling sitting down talking again. Georgina passed out, me following. Waking up I feel awful, I drank way too much, me and Georgina both laid on the sofa I can't remember most of last night, did Jessica leave?

"Can you remember Jessica leaving?" Looking at Georgina she shakes her head.

"I am off to bed; a couple of hours sleep is needed" we both walked into our own bedrooms. Texting Jackson I said I would speak to him later, texting Liam I explained it is safe to come home, lying down I fall asleep quickly again. A loud banging waking me up, groggily I roll out of bed to the door, opening it Jackson stood there.

"Where's Liam? He's ignoring texts from me and my mum" He walks past me, straight into Liam's room, coming back he looked scared.

"He texted me saying he was with you earlier, that was this morning" He replied to me, when I said it was safe to come home, he told me he was with Jackson.

"No Alena, I haven't seen him all week, where is he? When did you last see him?" He is panicking, and it is making me panic where is Liam?

"The last time I saw him was Friday, just before he went out, we had food and sat talking. But he replied to my text this morning, he also text Georgina as well" Calling Georgina she came out looking rather annoyed.

"Has Liam text you?" Jackson looked at her, waiting.

"Yes, yesterday morning, he just text saying he had left early, it was around six, why, what's wrong?"

"See, he sent us all a text" Grabbing my phone I show him, and he seems to relax a little.

"This is typical of Liam, having a weekend bender and hardly getting back in touch with anyone, our mum was worried sick when he didn't reply" He is explaining why he was so worried.

"Well, I'm going back to bed, my head is killing me, Jackson, you hurt her, I mean actually hurt her, I will kill you, just so you aware" She is glaring at him, turning she walks off into her room, he looks at me confused.

"It doesn't matter" Laughing at her and how confused he is.

"Well, come on I have a surprise for you today" Grabbing my hand, he walked towards the door pulling me with him.

"Wait, I am not even dressed, give me ten minutes and I will be ready" Walking into my room, I quickly get showered and dressed, walking out he smiles, grabbing my hand, leading me to the car, he drove for a bit, after fifteen minutes the route became familiar.

"Are we going back to Seductive Vibrations?" Looking at him confused, I have a feeling we are.

"I told you, I have a surprise for you, it's your choice if you want to accept it or not, but I think you'll like it" He is smiling, what has he got planned? I am not sure I like the idea of this at all, I am beginning to wonder if he's done what I think, is he really just trying to make my fantasy come true, if so, can I really go through with it? Staying quiet the rest of the drive was easy, my mind racing around screaming at me. Finally pulling up the small country road that leads to Seductive Vibrations, I smile, I love this place I really do.

4 LITTLE FANTASY

We pulled up to the beautiful Mansion also known as Seductive Vibrations, a dungeon as Jackson referred to it. Jackson takes my hand, leading me inside, we are walking briskly to his room, getting there he poured me a drink as I sat.

"Right, so I'm just going to tell you what your surprise is, I have planned something for you, if you don't want to do it, then you don't have to, I totally respect your decision. I will just enjoy the time with you. Your fantasy, well, I have a woman here waiting for you, I know you'll like her though" He looks at me, seeing the terror on my face, is he for real? Is he joking and trying to test me?

"Don't worry, this lady is a lot like you, you are her fantasy too, she's always wanted to be with a woman, but never has, and neither have you so it will help both of you relax. Honestly Alena, you don't have to do anything at all, you can just meet her and decide from there, I just thought it would be a nice surprise for you" I can meet her, see how things go then decide I don't have to agree instantly to do anything.

"Okay then, I'll meet her" I sound nervous, I am but I would hate myself for walking away without even meeting her.

"Do you want me to be with you or not?" Honestly, not, it is something I have to do alone, I don't think I could do something with a woman for the first time with him here, we have not exactly been together long enough to have that much confidence in front of each other, or rather I don't.

"I will be fine alone" Smiling at him, his body moving towards mine, his lips pressing against mine passionately, going to unbutton his shirt, his hands grasping mine, holding them together, his lips teasing me, kissing my neck stopping at my ear.

"There's something to remember me by, don't worry, you've got this, everything you might want or need it next to the bed" His lips starting to kiss me again, across my neck and down my chest moaning, he reached my breasts. He stood up smiling, walking out, me sitting here alone, a couple of minutes later a woman walked in, she was a few years older than me, she looks just as terrified as me, I feel like I have to say something to help her relax a bit, to reassure her that she was safe.

"Hi, I am Alena, come in and sit, we can just talk honestly" Smiling at her, she walked in sitting down, sitting here we just stay silent, I need to make some sort of effort to talk.

"So, I guess you don't have a partner?" Looking at her I smile, I hope not or if she does, he knows she is here.

"No, I am not really the sort to settle down with a partner to be honest, not yet anyway. Clearly you and Jackson are together?" Nodding in response to her question I smile.

"We are, we are new only been together about four weeks, but it is going well" She smiles, her mouth looks perfect.

"Are you okay with this?" Looking at me, her question confusing me.

"Yes, we spoke about fantasies, and things like that, this is his way of helping, he seems happy with me doing this" Sitting we spoke for a while, drinking what I believe is Jacksons stash of booze, laughing, we both relaxed, Roxy really is fun, she is quiet and as Jackson said she never was with a woman, never built up the courage to go out and find one. Sitting we spoke about our fantasies together, multiple fantasies we both have. She then also told me how she thinks Jackson is hot, I feel like I should be annoyed or Jealous but I'm not, not even a bit, I like her and the fact she likes Jackson just makes me like her more. Laughing I leant forward my lips pressing against hers, expecting her to push me away and say no, she didn't her lips starting to kiss back, my body going into shock, what have I just started? her hand raising up, her fingers running through my hair, her kiss so much different to Jackson, so different to any guy I have been with, soft and passionate, it feels amazing. I am going crazy for more, just like I do when Jackson kisses me, my leg wraps around her waist, pulling her towards me, moaning, still kissing her, my hands sliding up her top, over her breasts. Her lips moving along my jaw, down to my neck, kissing me, her lips running along my collar bone, she keeps kissing her mouth going lower, her body climbing on top of me, pushing me down on my back, her hands pulling her top off, bending down she starts kissing me again, reaching around I unfasten her bra, watching it fall. Sitting up, I begin pulling my top off, her hands wrapping around me, unfastening my bra, it is thrown on the floor, her hands pulling me closer to her, our breasts colliding. Her mouth kissing my neck again, pushing me back down on the bed, her lips moving down, finally finding my breasts, she is kissing them softly, her tongue gently stroking over the nipple, with one hand she starts playing with my breasts, the other unfastening my trousers. My hands begin to run down her body, feeling across her breasts, my fingers tingling from the touch, I love touching her soft warm skin. My hands playing with her breasts as she teased mine, reaching down the side of the bed she pulled up a blindfold.

"You first" She slipped it over my eyes, everything going dark, I can't say no, I want it. She started moving, his lips kissing my breasts moving down to my stomach, her hands pulling my pants and underwear down, her tongue trailing along my pubic bone, moaning from the sensation she kept moving down. Her tongue finding my entrance, starting to lick it gently, my hands grasping her hair, as her tongue worked faster, teasing around my clit, moving down her tongue pushing against my pussy, it is pure ecstasy, moaning I push my hips up towards her. Every second feels different, in an amazing way, her tongue moving quickly, as her hand tug my hard nipples, her mouth rising back to my clit, her finger teasing, rubbing gently against my pussy, the wetness growing, I can feel myself leaking with pleasure as her fingers just keep teasing outside. Pushing her fingers inside me, she makes us both moan with pleasure and anticipation, moving them in and out, her tongue still licking my clit, grabbing my legs, she pulls me down, her tongue sliding inside me, her hands holding me in place. I can't move, her tongue beginning to lick faster, enjoying my sweet taste, she is incredible, to think I was going to say no to this! Moaning from pleasure, her fingers pounding into my wet pussy, her hand starting to play with my nipples, nearly losing control, I am right on the edge. Her rhythm building up a combination of her fingers fucking me, her mouth licking my clit with her playing with my nipples sending me over the edge, feeling a release from the pleasure, it feels like a lightning bolt flowing through my body. Trying to close my legs, signaling I have cum, she obviously knows I have. Her hands, forcing them open, she moved, climbing on top of me, kissing my body until she reached my lips, her kiss against my lips, I can taste something strange, my own juices, feeling myself get turned on from it, her hands removing the blindfold. I moved quickly, rolling her over, my body sitting on hers, sliding the blindfold over her eyes.

Straddling her, my lips beginning to kiss her, slowly kissing all over her neck, then moving down to her collarbone, kissing slowly hearing her breathing race as I reached her breasts, just looking at them turns me on, gently I suck her nipple into my mouth, my teeth gently biting down. I feel so in my element, this feels better than her doing it to me. My kisses moving down her body, stopping between her legs, my heart racing, while I love this, should I do it? I can't not, I am loving every second. My tongue slowly rolling over her pussy, licking up to her clit and back down, taunting her with my slow antagonizing movements. My hands moving up, grabbing her breasts with my hands, my tongue digging deep inside her, her moans and screams making me wet, My tongue keeps moving at a steady rhythm until I can feel her close to the edge, reaching the edge I stop, reaching down the side of the bed, I pick up the nipple clamps and the whip, placing them on the bed, I swing the whip down, watching her back arch as she expresses her pleasure. This is driving me wild, my hand swings again the whip hitting down, her moans and screams louder, slowly my mouth sucks on her nipple, releasing it from my mouth, I clip the clamp on, watching as her body jumps from the shock, my mouth teasing her next nipple, pushing the clamp onto it, watching her jump from the pleasure. My hand running down her body, stopping at her pussy, slowly inserting my fingers and pulling them back out, purposely teasing her, watching her squirm trying to get closer. Removing my fingers, I push them in hard and fast, her yelp sending me wild, her body pushing down on my fingers, moving them out again, her voice begging for me to continue, I can see why Jackson loves this so much now. Swinging the whip, it hits across her clit listening to her moans of pleasure, making me climb right back up I am close to the edge myself just watching her pleasure. My fingers slide inside her, moving in and out fast and hard, my mouth lowering sucking on her clit, she tastes amazing, she is amazing, her moans making me moan with pleasure. Her body showing her pleasure as her wetness grew, her body changing, sensing she was close to the edge again, my fingers moving in and out rubbing the sides as I do, my tongue darting across her clit quickly. Her hands grasping my hair, holding me in place, her body shaking from pleasure as he climaxed, her juices running along my fingers, lifting them, I sucked the juices off, she tastes amazing, her body relaxing, I crawl upwards kissing her, her hands removing the blindfold, lying next to each other on the bed, we didn't say anything. Falling asleep, I woke hearing a light knock at the door. Sitting up I cover Roxy, she was not waking up.

"Yes" I call quietly hoping not to wake her. Jackson walks in looking at the glasses on the floor and empty bottle, his laughing sounding around the room.

"So, you got drunk and passed out? Don't worry, I am not mad, it just means you know her a bit better and maybe next time you will both feel confident enough to take the step" He walks towards the bed, noticing our clothes thrown on the floor

"Ah, maybe not" he looked at me intrigued, he clearly didn't expect me to do it. I now feel embarrassed this is not something I expected to do ever, fantasies are not often acted out.

"Did you both really drink all of that?" He leant down picking up the bottle.

"I drank most of it, she isn't a drinker really" I laugh, getting out of bed, throwing the gown on that was next to it, I don't understand why he is so shocked, it is only a bottle of whiskey.

"You do realise this is old, and strong really strong" He looked at me in disbelief, still confused by his shock.

"Whiskey is whiskey when you're building up

courage" Laughing I walked over to him, my arms wrapping around his neck, it feels strange cuddling him after everything I just did.

"Should we wake her?" Looking at Roxy asleep, I have no idea what the next step is, what are we meant to do now?

"No, just let her sleep, it's my private room so no one will come in, no harm with her sleeping. Are you hungry?" I had not even thought of food, but now he mentions it, I am hungry my stomach making noises.

"I am starving, I could just eat you right now" winking at him, pulling him to me, my kisses against his lips.

"For food, not me, food Alena" He laughed looking at me, shaking his head in disbelief.

"I am famished, so I should eat, let me grab some clothes" Walking around I picked up my clothes, putting them on, his eyes watching me, walking out we went down to the restaurant, I feel like everyone is staring at me, I am just being a little paranoid, sitting down at the same table as last time, we sat waiting for our good, Roxy coming over, standing at the table, she smiles waiting like me unsure what to do next.

"Hey Roxy" I smile at her, she is so cute.

"Want to join us for some food?" Jackson looked up at her. Her face is blushing, her eyes glancing at me, clearing remembering what happened, or maybe it's the fact she admitted to me she thought Jackson was hot? I honestly did not take offense and I won't tell him either.

"Come on, you may as well sit and enjoy some free food from Jackson while you're here" Laughing I moved over, my arm, pulling her onto the seat, she sat down, the awkwardness is creeping back in, I don't know what to say, I feel like I want to run away.

"So, Roxy, are you staying around here long? You mentioned you were just visiting?" Jackson looks rather interested to find out, I am pleased he was saying something, it meant the awkward feeling was slowly fluttering away.

"I think so, I'm just waiting to see how things go, to be honest. I don't really have a plan, I know it sounds crazy, but if I like this place, I may stay" She is smiling at him, the waiter walking back with our food. Sitting we ate talking about everything and anything. Jackson got called away, he walked off, leaving me and Roxy alone, I feel more relaxed than I did before.

"Thank you" Roxy smiled at me, looking at her shocked why would she be thanking me? She could clearly see my confusion.

"Thank you for making me feel relaxed, I like that I had a choice, like I could just enjoy myself and walk away without doing anything, I was afraid I would be made to stay or something" her confession making me smile, it kind of reminded me of the first day I came here.

"To be honest Roxy, when I first came here, I called Jackson a pimp" I burst out laughing remembering, Roxy joining in and laughing with me.

"He's never told me anything about his business before, he told me to keep an open mind, I didn't know what to expect. After seeing this place, I just jumped to the conclusion that he was a pimp" Sitting, I begin explaining why I thought that, so she would understand why.

"I know how you feel, I was worried because of the windows, I didn't want someone to watch, I like Jackson though, he's nice and he seems to understand people's worries and knows how to solve them" She was smiling, relaxing more it feels weird, I never expected to actually go through with this, yet somehow, I managed it.

"He explained it to me loads before I realised, the thing is though, how he explains it is perfect, but the thing that made me relax, then made me realise it was a nice place, everyone was smiling, all the guests happy, you can clearly see they can leave at will if they want and they feel safe. So how did you find out about this place?" She seems so shy, I can't help but wonder how she found it.

"A friend of mine works here, she had a girl's party, got talking about fantasies, she told me about this place. She told me when she was working and when she wasn't, so I could choose the best time, She's the one who spoke to Jackson for me. I was scared of just coming, I explained to her why, after she had told me she uses this place on her time off, so yeah, she helped because if it wasn't for her I doubt I would be here" She has me confused, why would the women just talk to Jackson about her? I don't have time to question though, Jackson is walking back towards us smiling, I will just leave it and remember to ask later I just find it weird the woman went to Jackson rather than just going through the normal way and booking her in like everyone else.

"What do you want to do now ladies? You know each other now and seem to get on, no fights or crying fits which is good, so are you swapping numbers and meeting away from here in the future? Yes, it's against the rules, but since it's me who made the rules, I guess I will bend them just this once" He laughs, how does he make people feel so comfortable just like that?

"We will exchange numbers" Smiling to Roxy I hold my phone out, her hand typing in her number, passing it back, she hands me hers, sitting there I type in my number. I hope we can meet up again, it is something I enjoyed.

"I will message you some time in the near future" Smiling I hug her.

"I should really leave, thank you Alena and thank you Jackson" Watching as she walked out the door, I can't help but smile, today was just amazing, nothing can destroy the mood I am in, I am glad Jackson took the lead and sorted this because I know if he didn't I would never have the guts to do it. Jackson was again called away by a worker, he walked off, grabbing the phone he stood talking, hanging up, he walked back towards me, his face full of worry.

"Has Liam messaged you yet?" He's looking at me and his worry is scaring me, grabbing my phone I unlock it.

"No, why? I'll phone Georgina and ask if she has heard from him" Calling Georgina it took a while for her to answer.

"Hey Alena, what's wrong?"

"Georgina, have you heard anything else from Liam?"

"No, nothing why?"

"I'm not sure, we will be home soon" Hanging up I look at Jackson his face full of worry, he is scaring me now.

"Try ring him Alena, he might answer to you, especially if he's just trying to cause trouble" His eyes watching me, please answer Liam, finding his number I hit call, sitting waiting, it is ringing, but no answer.

"He's not answering Jackson" I feel sick, I am worried now.

"Right, we have to go, we will go to the apartment first and see Georgina, we'll try and work out where he could have gone, and hopefully track him down" His hand pulling me up from the seat, I feel frozen, sitting in the car Jackson driving my mind on Liam, where is he?

"Why would he just go and not say anything? Where is he anyway?" Looking at Jackson he shakes his head, clearly having no idea either.

"I don't know, I thought maybe he would disappear to make me realise been with you hurt him, but this is too far, he wouldn't do this" I feel like this is my fault, what if he really isn't happy about me and Jackson? I feel worse because I should have insisted on finding him yesterday when he didn't show up, instead we just assumed he was having a mad weekend. Glancing at Jackson, I can't help but wonder if he blames me as well, getting into the apartment Georgina is waiting, looking worried.

"Anything?" I don't see why I asked that, if she had made contact she wouldn't look so worried, she just shook her head, walking in we sit down.

"Okay, which bars does he go to usually?" Jackson looked at Georgina, she would know more than me, I hardly ever go out. She sat listing names of bars and clubs, along with the people he usually goes out with. Sitting we ring around everyone one of them, each one saying they have not seen him.

"Right, so it looks like no one has seen him since Friday, but his friend Mark said he left with a woman Friday, so maybe he pulled?" Jackson shook his head, not accepting it as a good enough excuse.

"Even if he had, he would have answered his phone by now. Liam isn't one for keeping quiet either, I would have had a text by now from him bragging about pulling, actually I would have had one the night he pulled" He is worrying me now.

"Oh, before I forget, your jacket is over there Jackson" Georgina is pointing towards the jacket I had totally forgot about that, it is a good job she remembered but right now I doubt Jackson will care about where his jacket was.

"Erm, no that isn't mine, not my style at all" He is looking at us confused, so it isn't his jacket then

"Well, whose is it? As it certainly wouldn't fit Liam, you're the only other guy that comes here" Panic rising inside me, what the hell is happening?

"The door was unlocked remember, but I could have sworn I locked it. That jacket must have been put there during the night" Georgina pointed out, looking around, had someone else been in here while we slept?

"Alena, you don't think it was him, do you?" I don't need to look at her to know who she is talking about, bile beginning to rise inside me, looking up fear in my eyes would it be Max? What would he even gain from coming here and leaving his Jacket, just to try to scare me? I feel too hot, and every second I am getting worse, my heart beating faster, skipping beats from the fear.

"I don't want to think about Georgina, I don't want to even consider it being him" Tears streaming down my face, I can't deny it no amount of denying it, will make it not, it has to have been him, who else could it be?

"Alena, you have to accept the fact it might be him" Georgina pushing me to accept it.

"No, I have just started getting myself back, literally I have just felt happy and safe enough to leave the house alone, happy enough to find someone else and enjoy myself, I can't Georgina if he's back, I just can't" My words getting stuck as more tears begin to fall, Jackson falling on his knees in front of me.

"I have to admit, it's quite weird. How do we know it wasn't him? Alena, look at me" His hand cupping my chin, pulling my face up to look at him.

"No matter what, you won't go back there, you won't lose yourself I won't let you, just try to remember what happened Friday night, think Alena" Looking at him, I have to for Liam, nodding I agree, my thoughts going back to Friday.

"I remember Liam leaving to go out, I went to bed, woke up after the nightmare, I was texting you" Smiling at him remembering about it, it was those texts that led to him sorting out today.

"I fell asleep again, I woke up you sat next to me on the bed" Jacksons face filled with fear, he looks scared.

"Alena, who was next to you on the bed? Because it sure as hell wasn't me, I didn't come here that night, I was at work all night" Wait, if it wasn't him, I feel dizzy, my heart is racing to quick, I am going to pass out, this can't be happening already, I knew we should have been worried when my stepmum came, I just hid my head and acted like it would be fine.

Like Max wouldn't come here to get me, clearly I was lying to myself.

"Alena, please kitten, try and remember, did you see their face, hear their voice? Anything at all you can remember?" Looking at him I feel sick, why did I not wake up fully why did I not question who it was?

"I thought it was you, I honestly did, I woke up hearing you saying something like fantasies do come true, I was too tired to do anything, I just fell straight back to sleep, I honestly thought it was you Jackson, I swear I did" My voice is frantic, I can't think about this, what would I have done had he tried kissing me? Would I have realised and stopped him or let him kiss me?

"Who the hell was in my bedroom and how did they know what you and I had discussed?" I am freaking out, my eyes glancing down at the phone in my hands, he's hacked my phone he has to have. Throwing it across the room, I scream.

"He's spying on me, I thought the rose and the note were from you, where the hell is Liam?" I am losing my mind, he has Liam, he has to have.

"Alena, calm the hell down, this won't help. Georgina pass me the note" Jacksons voice demanding, sitting down I feel like everything is my fault, Max is back, he has obviously done something with Liam, I can't stop the panic from rising inside me, Georgina walks back into the room, Jackson taking the note and looking at it.

"This was not from me Alena" Jackson put the note on the table, I kind of guessed that when he said he hadn't been here.

"Sorry, did you really need to read it just to confirm it wasn't from you? Could you not have just said I didn't leave you a note, and it wasn't from you" My words are cold, I flinch at them myself, I am terrified, and I am taking it out on him, he didn't respond, clearly seeing I am scared.

"Is Max the sort of person to hurt Liam?" Really, is he that stupid to ask, he knows what he did to me, surely, he knows that he is, I need to answer, without shouting at him.

"Yes, I guess if he thought I was with him, but we're not, so I don't know why he'd hurt Liam, why would he take Liam if he wants me?" I can't understand it at all, why would he take Liam if he wants me? I feel awful, I have put Liam in danger, I should have just stayed away from everyone.

"If max has been watching the apartment, he would have seen you and Liam leave together, he might assume you are together, you do laugh and joke a lot to the outside world they might see a couple" I hate her for being right, right now she is me and Liam are close, people always assumed we were together in university even Daz thought we were together, we aren't but clearly it is possible to think it and it is possible Max thinks it.

"I'm calling the police" Jackson walked out, we can hear his voice from the other side of the door.

Sitting here me and Georgina just stay quiet, my mind processing the whole thing, I hate myself right now for causing this.

"They're on the way, you need to try and remember if it was him in your room Alena" Jackson voice soft, his arms wrapping around me trying to comfort me, I am past being comforted, I am past getting over this without being hurt, the thought of Liam stuck with Max is scaring me, how can today end so badly? The start was amazing, I honestly didn't think anything would make me lose the happiness I had, well this certainly has.

"He wants me" My voice loud, realisation hitting me, Georgina and Jackson looking at me confused, how can they be confused it is obvious.

"Right and what does that have to do with anything?" Jackson is looking at me wondering why I would say it.

"He wants me, that's the way of getting Liam back" Jacksons face full of shock, his head shaking.

"No, you're not giving yourself over to him to try save Liam" Looking at him in disbelief, I can't not argue.

"Are you crazy, it is the quickest way to get Liam back, sure he will get me, but at some point, he will anyway, may as well do it now and get Liam back. You would honestly leave your brother with someone like him, rather than giving me up to save him? He is your brother" Georgina is looking at me like I have lost my mind, I haven't it is simple and easy that is how we get him back.

"Not a chance, and stop talking like he will get you, he won't while ever I am around, we are not trading you for him. Liam is bigger, he can take a lot more than you without breaking, you're already pretty fucked without going back there" He meant it, but I am not giving in that easily, his words hurt, am I really fucked?

"You would choose me over your brother? That is pretty fucked up Jackson, even I would choose him over me" I can't believe he is willing to leave Liam with Max knowing what he is capable of.

"Enough! No Alena, you're not swapping fucking places, the police will deal with it, I am sure Liam can take more hits than you can. Now shut up with the idea of turning yourself in, you're not" Okay, so he is set against me doing it, I can't argue with him, he is right, it is crazy, but I would do it for Liam, he doesn't deserve any of this.

"Sorry for snapping, but we can't guarantee you swapping places will save Liam, I don't want to lose you, and if we try to swap, how do we know he still won't hurt Liam believing you are together" He looks at me apologetically. I know I have to try something, anything but if I mention it, he will stop me, sitting quietly, I don't say anything else, grabbing my laptop, Jackson watches I open Facebook, searching I find his profile, clicking the message button, taking a deep breath I begin typing.

"Max, where is Liam? What is it you want, seriously, I just want Liam home safe" Sitting waiting for his reply, it doesn't seem to be coming, the police arrive, taking the note and Jacket, asking questions after questions, but I am useless, I was too tired to even realise it was not Jackson, the police left, and nothing was really done, they said they would search for him but honestly if it is Max he will be hidden somewhere.

"Georgina, are you okay here with Alena while I get a few guys and look for him myself? Keep the door locked and the key in the lock" He looked at her.

"Sure, you might as well go Jackson, you'll me more useful than the police, I won't let her leave" She is smiling but clearly hurting.

"I will find him Alena" Jackson kneeling in front of me his lips kissing me, standing up he took out his phone dialing a number and lifting it to his ear.

"Marcus, I need your help" His voice disappearing through the door as he left, Georgina locking it behind him. Sitting back down, she put the tv on, the noise was not really helpful, sitting here doing nothing is not helpful, grabbing my phone I sit back down, nothing, no reply at all from Max, what does he want, why won't he reply? Sitting we stay quiet for so long, my phone buzzing, picking it up expecting it to be Jackson, a message from an unknown number.

"Meet me here, be alone" The message has a map attached, opening it, I know where to go, Georgina is looking at me, expecting an update.

"Nothing yet, he said he'll keep us updated though, so not to worry" Sitting back, I get comfy, my mind taking a mental note of the address, surely, she needs to leave me alone soon. Waiting for what seems like ages, she finally got up, walking into the toilet, grabbing my coat I snoop out, heading straight for the address, running most of the way, I can only hope Liam is okay. Arriving outside the building looking in, I feel a sense of danger, of course there is going to be danger, it is Max, should I really do this, should I just wait and tell Jackson, but if he sees Jackson I have no idea how he will react. Bracing myself, I push open the doors, walking inside, pure blackness, walking further inside, I can't help but shake, I can't see a thing, my eyes are trying to adjust but there isn't enough light to. Walking in a feel like I have been walking at least a minute and still not reached anyone or a light.

"Alena, Alena" My body running towards the voice, no, stopping I remember this, it is my dream, I now know that man in the dream is Liam, I also know something hurts me and knocks me out, if I go in I may never get out again. I have to try to help him, though, scared I walk forward towards the voice, I can't see anything, it feels like this room never ends, fear crippling me as I get deeper inside Max's lure. Finally, my eyes can see a dark figure on the floor, stepping closer I catch a glimpse of his face, Liam, my eyes light up seeing him, somebody grabbing me from behind making me scream, kicking I try to escape, but I can't, something sharp digging into me, falling to the floor in pain, crawling to Liam, he looks a mess, this is my fault, Max has done this to him, turning, bracing myself to come face to face with Max for the first time in years, I can't let him win. I need to face him, show him I am not afraid of him anymore. Turning I see my attacker, my body going into shock, it isn't Max, it isn't even a man.

"Jessica, what on earth are you doing?" Why is she here?

"Alena, how come you're calling her Jessica?" Liam's voice quiet, his eyes looking at me confused.

"This is Jessica, Daz's girlfriend, I don't get it what did we do, I thought we got along great!" Is this all because Daz likes me? It seems a little crazy, but why else would she be here trying to hurt us? She moved closer to me, leaning down.

"Alena, move away from her" Looking at Liam, I don't get it what is going on? Turning back to face her, her spit hitting me in the face.

"You slept with my fiancé!" Her scream loud, I am confused, who the hell is her fiancé?

"I have not been near Daz if that is who you mean, I don't even know who your fiancé is" What have I done? She is laughing, so loud like I am crazy. Liam is trying to pull me closer to him, I can't move back, I need to know what I have done, his arm pulling me hard.

"It's Caroline" His voice quiet, her eyes shooting at him, yet when she looked at him, she has remorse, her eyes flicking back to me full of hate and anger. Caroline is Jacksons ex they were engaged, I actually feel sorry for her.

"Caroline, I am sorry, I had no idea it was you" I need to try explaining, what do I say?

"You slept with him, I've been watching you both, I should just kill you and get it over and done with" She really is crazy, I mean like crazy, crazy, I thought Max was, but this is just a whole new level.

"Jackson wouldn't forgive you if you did, he still loves you Caroline, I can see it when he told me about what happened with Tallulah" My voice quiet, trying to reason with her, he did still love her, how much I don't know, but even I could tell he did, watching her face twist, I realise mentioning Tallulah was the worst thing I could possibly do.

"Don't you ever mention my daughter's name again" She was angry, worse than before, picking me up, she threw me across the room, my body hurts so much I can barely breath, I can feel the blood running down my side, my hand holding where it hurts, realising she has stabbed me, crap this is where I die. Laughter escaping my lips, I can't stop it, I have gone from being beaten by someone I loved and hating it, to enjoying being tied up, and now I am about to die with Liam tied up, the irony. Her head turned, her glare telling me she is ready to rip my head off, Liam looking at me like I am crazy, maybe I am, maybe this was what was needed to tip me over the edge, to make me go as crazy as she is, if I am going down I may as well make it good.

"If you wanted Jackson that much, why did you hide? Why did you watch us get closer and closer why didn't you just show yourself and take him?" She is a fool, I won't sit quietly while she hurts me

"You think you're special because he took you to his business, because he showed you Seductive Vibrations, No Darling, he takes all his little fucks there" Her words cold, I wonder if it is true.

"What the hell is Seductive Vibrations?" Liam looking at us both waiting for an answer, well Jackson has no choice but to tell Liam about it now. Now my mind is wondering was Jackson saying the truth when he said there was no one after Caroline?

"Why would you take Liam, he is Jackson's brother do you not think you have hurt Jackson enough with Katie? Now you're planning to hurt his brother" My eyes looking into hers, I don't care if I make her angry now.

"No, I don't want to hurt Liam, I have not laid a finger on him, I didn't mean to hurt Katie, that was an accident, I really did love her like a sister" Looking at her, I can't help but feel sorry for her, I can't help but feel her pain she honestly didn't want to hurt Katie.

"Caroline, I am here, so just leave go get Jackson back if you want him that much, You know he's out looking for Liam right now, if you wait too long he won't ever come back to you" I mean it's nice, clearly she doesn't think so her body lunging at me, her fists hitting me over and over, my arms trying to protect me as best as I can, okay so I can't mention Jacksons name or Liam's or anyone's because she gets angry.

"You don't think I already know that, I need to get rid of you first so there's no way he'd be able to look at you again" She is moving away from me, my body hurts, I can hardly move, looking around the windows are all boarded up. She sits in front of us, just watching, looking at Liam I want to comfort him, say sorry for being such a shitty friend.

"I didn't want to do this, I honestly thought you would see what he was like and decide that isn't for you, I sat smiling when I followed you to Seductive Vibrations for the first time, waiting for you to run, then you didn't you actually stayed there all night" Her head is shaking as she tries to work out what she should say next.

"Then I realised, he is willing to hide himself for you, keep that part of his life hidden from you, that was not the issue. The issue is, I can see it in you, you will give him what he wants and needs unlike me and there will be no way I can win him back then" She looks hurt, scared and angry, why do I feel sorry for her when she is doing this. Sitting there she looks up to Liam.

"Tell him I am sorry, for what I am about to do, for Katie and for leaving" Liam looks at her shocked, is she going to leave?

"I will, just walk away and I will tell him Caroline, then you have a chance of getting him back" Liam's voice soft, she smiles at him, a menacing laugh escaping her twisted smile.

"You think I am going to let her go? No, that is why I said say sorry for what I am about to do" Standing up she walked closer to him.

"I really did feel like part of the family" She turns looking at me and starts walking off.

"Don't even think about trying to get out, I'm coming straight back" She turned walking away quickly, struggling over to Liam, I pull him.

"Can you get free Liam?" Looking at him he didn't move, so I am guessing not.

"No, I have been trying all weekend, she put something in my drink, she brought me here. I remember her saying something about Jackson being hurt, I woke up chained like this" Looking around I can't see anything, I can't find anything to use.

"Get out Alena, Get out now! It's you who she wants to hurt, so run" His hand rubbing my cheek gently, he was right, she won't hurt him, she doesn't want to hurt Jackson and hurting Liam would. Struggling to my feet I stumble forward, my legs trying to carry the dead weight of my body, my whole body is hurting, I won't make it, I know I won't the front is too far away, struggling forwards I keep going, I can make it, I need to make it,

"Alena, look out!" Jackson's voice loud something hitting me, my body falling to the floor. Caroline stood there, a brick in her hand, ready to throw it at me, Jackson grabbing her, pulling her to the floor, his arms wrapping around her.

"I am sorry, I just didn't want to lose you, I know you still love me" Caroline's voice quiet, Jacksons face full of love and hate.

"I did, I did Caroline, I loved you so much for Tallulah, I told myself I would forgive you for Katie, I told myself it was an accident and forgave you, but this is no accident, you're not the person I loved, that love has gone" My eyes feeling heavy, someone pulling me off the floor.

"Check her Marcus, her back looks like it's bleeding" Someone checking my body, I can feel his hands, is that the Marcus he spoke to?

"I thought you would hate me" Caroline's voice sad and broken.

"I couldn't hate you, we made Tallulah together, I loved you, but I can't love you for what you are now" My eyes closing, the pain is awful, my last memory, Jackson cradling Caroline as she broke into tears. Waking up dazed, the room is far too bright, panicking, I try moving, my body restrained down, I wasn't saved, I can't have been where has she brought me now? Jackson must have just been a dream, my imagination trying to make me think I have survived and escaped. My body thrashing, the pain unbelievable, screaming a mixture of fear and pain.

"Calm down Alena, look at me" Jackson's voice quiet, turning I can see him, he looks awful like he has been crying and not slept for weeks, my whole-body hurts, I need to sit up, why can't I sit up, pulling against the straps I scream, why am I the one tied down?

"Stop freaking out, if you do, they'll unstrap you, they expected you to freak out after what happened, the shock taking over" He is moving, his body walking towards me. My body relaxing seeing him closer to me, his hand grasping mine, his thumb stroking over it, looking up to him his head fell.

"I'm sorry Alena, this is my fault, I am so, so sorry" The nurses looking at him, he nodded as they started unfastening the straps. His words on replay in my head, I am so, so sorry.

"I knew, I could see it when you spoke about her, you love her, that isn't going to leave, I will be fine, you love Caroline, you should be with her" He is looking at me like I am crazy.

"What are you talking about?" Sitting next to me, he waits for my answer.

"You love Caroline, I saw it when you spoke of her, I heard you saying how you told yourself to forgive her, how you love her, I understand Jackson" I need to say goodbye, move on and hope I recover quickly from it at least he has shown me I can be myself again, I will find a way to be myself without him.

"No Alena, no, I don't even think a thousand no's

would be enough, I love you, any love I had for her has gone, I am not walking away Alena, I was saying sorry because you being hurt is my fault" Relief flooding through my veins I honestly thought I had lost him, jumping up to hug him, I scream, the pain is unreal, falling back onto the bed,

"Stay still, you're still seriously hurt" The nurse's voice quiet, trying to calm down so that the nurses would finally leave so we could have some privacy, they finally did, looking up at Jackson with confusion on my face.

"What happened?" My mind trying to remember, but I can't did I pass out at the point where he was saying he loved her?

"Apparently Caroline has been watching me for years, from time to time she would watch Liam, she saw us together and realised we were dating, she made friends with Daz, and used him as a way to get to you" His eyes looking at me.

"She was obviously the person who broke into your apartment, she denies it, she even denied doing this to you though, you left your phone so when Georgina noticed you were gone, she looked at it seeing the address, she rang me and we headed straight for you" His eyes looking at me ready for the next piece.

"What you did was crazy, stupid and crazy, I came close to losing you Alena, and I would have hated that, I really would have" His head lowers, his pain showing on his face.

"I arrived, I saw her behind you with a pole in one hand and brick in the other, I shouted you, but it was too late, I grabbed her, Marcus grabbed you and the police were called, I was cradling her yes, because for the first time she cried, she never cried when Tallulah passed away, she just stayed quiet, she was grieving, I couldn't let her grieve for our daughter alone, Liam is okay, Caroline is now locked up" I can't blame him for that, I wouldn't blame him if he still loved her.

"I don't blame you for comforting her, I honestly don't she didn't mean to hurt Katie, even I could tell that, she was clearly too scared to face you, too scared you would reject her so she hid" Why am I defending her, she tried to kill me.

"She stabbed you through your side, and your face, well isn't as beautiful as it was" He joked, winking at me.

"I am kidding it is, of course it is. You're just very swollen at the moment, she hit you and split your head open, so you have quite a lot of battle wounds" His face etched with pain.

"I'm so sorry, all of this is because of me, I was the one who agreed that It must have been Max, I should have thought that it could be her, I just don't understand why now? Why after all these years? I am so sorry Alena, if you would have died, I would never have forgiven myself" Trying to move to him, I try to cuddle him, the pain is too much, radiating throughout my torso.

"Come here you idiot" I beckoned.

"It's not your fault at all, maybe I should have just told you the address then it wouldn't have happened, and she did it now because she had clearly realised you were getting closer to me than she liked, she didn't want to lose you" His eyes softened, his head beginning to shake.

"Why are you defending her, she was going to kill you Alena" Looking at him, he really doesn't understand does he, I may not have kids, or being pregnant but I am not blind to the pain she is going through.

"I don't see her as Caroline, I see her as the women who lost her baby, who crashed her car and killed Katie, I see her as a broken woman, just like me all those years ago, sure I didn't hurt anyone, I was still broken though, and she clearly is. I see your pain when Tallulah is mentioned, just because she is crazy doesn't mean she doesn't feel the same pain as you, or any other person grieving for their child, I can't ignore that no matter how much she hurt me, I could clearly see she was hurting" His smile widened, and there it was the pain from Tallulah, he can't hide it he can try but I can see it in his eyes.

"You're too kind, honestly Alena, but I understand what you mean" His lips pressing against mine, kissing him back, I don't feel anything, no spark, no magnets drawing us together nothing.

"You're awake" Georgina is squealing running into the room, her arms wrapping around me tight.

"Ouch!" My scream loud from the pain, her body jumping back.

"I'm sorry, I'm just glad to see you awake finally" She is smiling, clearly happy, Liam stood by the door just looking at me.

"Thank you for coming to save me, or at least trying to save me" His smile small, his head lowered, I would have done it again in a heartbeat.

"Please can everyone leave, she needs to recover too many people will delay it" The nurse is standing at the door waiting for them to leave, Georgina and Liam say goodbye and walk out, Jackson standing here looking at her defiant, he isn't going anywhere, sensing it she gives up walking out. She is right, I am exhausted and fell asleep quickly, waking up I wouldn't be awake for long before falling back to sleep, my body drifting in and out of consciousness for days. Waking up Jackson sitting on the side of the bed.

"You can come home today" He is smiling yet the guilt is still evident on his face.

"You're coming to mine, okay, no arguing" He stood strong, to be honest though I would rather be with him than anywhere else, but at the same time I am worried about Liam and Georgina.

"Will they be okay?" Looking at him I need reassurance.

"If your meaning Georgina and Liam, then yes. It was all Caroline, you have nothing at all to worry about now. She is locked up and I am sorry for what she put you through because of me" I can't help but smile, but at the same time I feel scared, now what happens, surely he will have to see her again, he can't just walk away and pretend like she never existed. I can't keep thinking about it, I have to just forget it after the past few days, all I should be doing is concentrating on recovering, getting better and becoming me again. Thinking into things won't help at all.

"Okay, I will come to yours" He is smiling seemingly happy about it, I won't pry or ask questions about Caroline, I can't expect him to just walk away from her. He is being too kind, like he is trying to make up for what has happened, helping me get ready I hurt all over and I can only wonder if he is only doing this because he feels guilty.

"I will take the bags down, sit and wait for me to come back up and I will help you get your coat on" He walks out, sitting after a couple of minutes I can't just wait slowly getting my coat on Georgina walks in smiling.

"You're finally coming home, where are all your things?" She starts looking around the room trying to find my bags, but she won't.

"Jackson took them, he said I am staying with him for a while, he has just gone to put the bags in the car, then he's coming back for me" I assumed she would already know, but clearly not, she walks out in a huff, sitting waiting they take ages to come back, clearly, they are arguing over where I am staying. Ten minutes later the door opens, Georgina walking through with Jackson right behind her.

"Okay, so we have been discussing what would be best for you, you can come home there will be me and Liam to look after you, so two people not one. We can take time off university to help you. Jackson is of course more than welcome to stay over. Or you can go with Jackson where there is just him" She is saying it like she is disgusted with him, I can't help but laugh though, the whole me and Liam or just Jackson. I don't like the fact she is trying to force me to decide between them Jackson just sat quietly, not getting involved.

"I'm not a child, I can decide for myself, and I already decided I want to go and stay with Jackson. I know that I can leave and come back home at any time if I want to, if I get bored of him, I will come home to be entertained" I am joking, I highly doubt I will get bored with Jackson, but you never know, Georgina is smiling so I take it she agrees, Jackson looking smug that he won, he only won because he didn't stand there telling me my options like I was a child.

"Can I leave now? I've been stuck in here for ages" I look at them for confirmation, I would have been out ages ago if they didn't have a disagreement.

"Sure, I will call round sometime to see you throughout the week, if that's okay?" I can see the glare she threw at him, what have I missed? I won't ask, I will just wait no doubt one of them will say, Jackson helped me to the car, driving to his house, it feels weird being back here, the openness of the place is scary, remembering anyone can see in my eyes, looking into the kitchen, the spot where we first had sex, was she watching us then? How long has she been watching us, I am now thinking being here isn't such a good idea after all.

"I can close the blinds Alena, I've told you, you don't have to worry, she is locked up, you'll never have to see her again" He is walking around, the blinds closing, walking into the living we sit down, I can't do it I need to ask.

"So, what happens now?" Looking at him I wait, I need to know his plans.

"We wait until you're better, then try and get back to normal as much as possible" Smiling, his lips press against mine, moving back he is still smiling.

"Jackson, that's not what I mean, are you saying you won't see Caroline again? You're not even slightly interested in making sure she is okay?" He honestly just can't ignore all this, yet I want him to say he won't see her, the fact he loves her scares me even if he says he doesn't you can't just turn off love like a switch.

"Okay, honestly, yes, I am going to see her, not because I love her, or to make sure she is okay, I am going to tell her the day she killed Katie and ran away, she ended our relationship. The day she hurt you, I lost all love for her, and there is no going back for us now, sure had she walked back in and apologised sincerely, then maybe, I know that will hurt to hear, but she didn't. She is not the Caroline I fell in love with all those years ago" That hurts, knowing that he had me here, at his work when in the back of his mind he knew he would take Caroline back if she walked into his life. It makes me wonder if he loves me, I feel I love him yet knowing Caroline meant more than me, I don't think I can cope with that.

"I'm tired, where am I going to be sleeping?" I don't want to talk anymore about Caroline, I knew he loved her I just didn't think he would have started a relationship with me knowing he would take her back. I spent a week in a hospital bed, and now I wish I was still in it.

"Your choice, you can sleep with me if you like, or in one of the guest rooms" He is looking at me, waiting for my answer, why has that pull for him gone, it seems to no longer exist, the fact is, I don't want to upset him or make him feel worse he already blames himself, I also don't want to sleep alone.

"With you, of course" Smiling at him, he nods, he isn't a fool he can see things have changed in my mind. He began helping me upstairs, showing me his room, it is beautiful, walking around looking at it, I feel calm and relaxed, he brings in my bags, then walks out leaving me to get sorted. Climbing into the bed, lying here my mind is trying to get used to the idea of how much life has changed, the most important point, is why do I no longer feel attracted to Jackson, I don't have that urge to rip off his clothes, I literally feel nothing for him, the worry is unreal, what happens if I never feel that way again, I can't stay with someone I can't connect with, I just found someone who makes me feel like me, makes me wild and free and just like that the connection has gone. Sleep swept me away, my thoughts turning into dreams. Waking Jackson isn't next to me, I am guessing it is still day time, slowly I climb out of bed, ignoring the pain, walking downstairs finally reaching the bottom, stopping to catch my breath I can hear Jackson.

"How can they believe it was not an accident, so what happens now is she being released?" He sounds angry, pausing to listen to whatever is being said.

"Well, I guess that will have to do. I have told Alena, she can't hurt her, so you need to make sure she stays there, Katie wasn't an accident not at all, the speed the fact she headed for that wall. I don't care what she says, is what she did with Liam and Alena enough to keep her there?" I feel awful sitting here listening, especially when it is about Katie, I should move, walking down, the next step, I try to make noise, so he knows I am walking down the stairs.

"Okay, that will do thank you and keep me updated" He hung up the phone turning to me smiling.

"Just in time, food is almost ready, and Georgina is on her way to check on you" He came over, helping me to sit at the table, Georgina walking in she smiled, I wish I had her life, so uncomplicated and pain free.

"I spoke to Daz, he feels awful about what happened, he feels partly responsible, he is also gutted his girlfriend wasn't a real one" I feel awful, he got dragged into it.

"He doesn't need to feel bad, it isn't his fault at all"

"So, how are you?" She looks at me then Jackson, he smiles and walks off leaving us alone.

"Seriously Alena, what happened? I know something has you don't look at Jackson the same way even Liam noticed" I wish I knew, I don't know what is going on, not at all.

"I don't know, before I passed out, I saw Jackson cradling Caroline, I am fine with it, but he said he loved her" My mind replaying it.

"I saw his love for her, his pain that he shares with her, then he told me, had she just came back, he would have taken her back, so maybe I was wrong thinking he felt more for me, I just don't feel anything" She is looking at me with sympathy like I have lost someone close to me, maybe I have, it certainly feels that way.

"So why are you here, leave come home, don't put yourself through more pain Alena" Her words make sense, but I can't I just can't walk away from him yet, I can't bring myself to say goodbye.

"I can't, I am hoping it is the shock of everything, and in a couple of days I feel how I used to, if not then I will walk away, I promise" I have to, I can't sit around and wait just in case I feel the same again. Sitting we spoke for a while longer before she left. The next two weeks were slow, my body getting better, I have not left the house at all, my body now no longer hurts, which is great, sitting with Jackson we are eating, I still feel nothing, not even a thing for him, why? I think it is now time to accept facts, it is over, I can't fool myself anymore and I have seen his face, he can say things have changed, my feelings have changed for him.

"I think I should go home now, I am able to look after myself, I have recovered and I'm not in pain anymore, so I will be okay alone" Smiling at him, this breaks my heart, I feel like I love him, but at the same time I can't because I feel like I am being blocked, he clearly could sense it as he has barely touched me, a quick hug and kiss here and there but nothing else.

"If you want to, that's fine. But I want you this weekend I want to introduce you to my mum. We are going to the grave on Sunday, it's the day Katie died, I would love for you to join us" He is looking at me, so much pain in his eyes, how can I say how I am feeling now, I would look heartless. I will do this, and then tell him and walk away.

"Of course, I'd love to come and support you" How can I meet him mum knowing I don't even know if I like him anymore, sure I like him but not like before. His head bent down, his lips kissing me, closing my eyes, I try to relax, try to feel anything, his lips pressing against my neck.

"I wouldn't be here today, you realise that, if you didn't make it I wouldn't be here. When I saw her hit you, I felt it, somehow I felt the pain and I wanted to take it away from you" His voice soft against my ear.

"That was when I realised I fucking love you, how you got me so quick I don't know, But I do. Honestly, I know what I said about Caroline, but I know now I would not have walked away from you if she came back, I don't know what you have done, but you have me hooked, and I really do love you" My body relaxed, my heart racing, his head moving back, looking at me, I can feel it again, I feel the magnet that draws me to him, my mind free, the worry that he loves Catherine gone. His lips pressing against mine, my mind racing, I can't stop myself, realising that I have missed him, I hadn't let him love me for the past two weeks, I have had my shield up protecting myself. His hands lifting me up, my legs wrapping around him as he carried me back upstairs, his lips pressing against mine. Laying me down, he began taking the clothes off, this feels weird, looking at my scar I can't do it, pulling the sheet up over my body, my arms pulling him to me, trying to hide the scar. He took his time, his hips moving slow, his eyes filled with love, I felt this before with him, but this time it feels so different, he's letting his guard down, lying here after, the sex was so different, he wasn't just fucking me like he always does, as much as I love that side of him, the chains, whips and everything else, I love this side even more. I feel like he was showing me he loved me, he was so gentle and careful, constantly kissing my lips, somehow it has made me fall in love with him more. He rolls onto his side, looking down at me smiling.

"You're amazing, there is something I don't know what. Just something tells me that if you walk away, I wouldn't stay, I don't think I can see my life without you, Alena. I love you" His confession bringing a tear to my eye, his words shocking me, I didn't realise he felt like I did, I assumed until today he liked me, not loved, just liked, looking at him, I can't help but wonder if we are moving too fast, is it a good or bad thing moving so fast, but I guess I should confess myself.

"You know that time on the doorstep, there was something there. I was praying you'd kiss me, I didn't want you to walk away" Looking at him smiling I carry on.

"You do something to me, I don't know how to explain it. I've never felt it before, I can be calm and relaxed and then you just look at me, and somehow I lose my mind, all rationality just flutters away, all I can do is think about you" His lips press against mine, moving back he looks at me.

"I trust you 100%, I don't even trust Liam or Georgina that much, I tried explaining how I felt to

Georgina and she doesn't understand, it's like I'm completely and utterly intoxicated by you, and I've felt it from the very start. I feel like I've loved you since the first moment I saw you, I just never expected you to choose me. The fact you somehow straight away pulled the real me out, made me feel like myself just makes me love you more" Looking at him, waiting for him to respond I only hope my confession has not made him want to run.

"We're just two messed up people that fit together perfectly, like two puzzle pieces, we're different designs, but we fit perfectly" His words sting a bit, he said I was fucked before and now he thinks I am messed up, he thinks he I'm messed up? Then again, thinking of my life, I guess I am in some ways, my mind hasn't been right since I was a child, After Max, I'd accepted I would never be the same again.

"You know, if I could go back and change my life, I wouldn't. I know it sounds crazy, the fact I would willing feel the hurt I felt as a child, the hurt Max inflicted on me, even Caroline, I know it sounds crazy, the fact if I went back and was given the option, I wouldn't say no, I wouldn't run, I would choose the exact same path. To me, it brought us together, and closer, I've realised that even though I'm broken or messed up, I can still be happy" Lying we just cuddle, not saying anything.

"Jack, where are you?" We both look up at the sound of Liam's voice.

"Come on Liam, you know exactly where he is"

Georgina's loud mouth travelling up the stairs.

"I guess it's time for us to move" Jackson bent down kissing my lips.

"Hey, wait a minute, so does everyone call you Jack or what?" I am curious.

"No, Liam does, he knows I hate the name Jack, it was my dad's name, I would rather people call me Jackson" He slid off the bed, handing me my clothes, we get dressed walking downstairs together, smiling like nothing has happened.

"Did you forget Jack, or were you just hoping that I would?" Liam staring at Jackson waiting for an answer, Jackson looks so confused.

"Well," He looked towards me, his eyes telling me I know what he is talking about.

"Don't act like you don't know, because I know you do" Looking at him, then Jackson it dawned on me, he was talking about Caroline mentioning Jackson's business.

"I think you need to discuss that with Jackson not me, I have nothing to do with his business. Seductive vibrations is nothing to do with me, Just because Caroline mentioned that I visited with him, doesn't mean I need to explain" Shrugging my shoulders, I am not getting involved. Jackson looking shocked at me, he is looking at me like I said something wrong.

"Caroline mentioned the business?" He looked at me, I totally forgot to warn him about it, actually I totally forgot about the whole thing.

"Well, thank you Alena for that reminder, however, I was talking about his birthday, it's today! But yeah, I definitely want to know about this business Caroline seemed so offended about because you took Alena" Liam looked at him, Jackson shaking his head, whoops, I guess Liam had forgotten for now as well.

"You're a child, you act like a child and my business isn't for children" He isn't going to tell him.

"You can either tell me, or I'll go visit Caroline and ask her" Ouch, low blow there Liam.

"Fine, come with me and I will explain" He started turning, walking away, going to follow him Georgina did as well.

"You two can stay here, I am sure you'll be able to tell Georgina about it a lot better than I can" He walks off, going into his office Liam following shutting the door, leaving me with Georgina of all people.

"What the hell is Seductive Vibrations? But before you answer that, what is happening, you said you was going to walk away Alena" She doesn't miss a trick, does she.

"I was, but I don't know things changed, and I feel like I did before the accident, I feel a lot stronger for him, and he said he loves me" Smiling remembering his words this morning.

"It wasn't an accident, stop saying it like that, but I am glad you feel he loves you. Now what the hell is Seductive Vibrations?" She stands waiting, I hate

Jackson for this, it should be me telling Liam and him dealing with Georgina.

"Look, if I have to tell you, I'm going to need a drink, you need to keep your mouth shut and your mind open, your opinions to yourself" Maybe I am a little bit too blunt, but I don't want to deal with her thinking it is wrong, grabbing a drink, I sit down, here goes.

"Right, so walking in, it is beautiful honestly, more beautiful than his house, walking upstairs there is halls you can go down, walking down with Jackson, there is windows, showing into the rooms"

"Each room was different with different people in them, somewhere just two women having sex, others were, well, one woman and several men, honestly, I called him a pimp, but then I realised that he isn't. All the people there are guests, not workers, the workers literally clean the rooms and look after guests" Looking up to her, her face is priceless, a perfect picture of someone in shock, I look at her and realise her face is mirroring what mine was when I first saw naked women in the rooms behind the windows.

"The place is safe and most importantly, it is legal. It's a business, but nobody pays, it's not like they're paying for sex. They don't at all, it's a place where people can go and act out their hidden fantasies, a place a lot of people go even with their partners" Looking at her, it just made her look more shocked, she never understands.

"I don't get it, so the people who work there don't have sex with the guests they don't get paid?" Yes, she is more confused.

"No, the staff do not sleep with the guests, yes staff gets paid obviously it is a job, but no one at all pays for sex, and none of the guests get paid for sex" She is struggling to understand this.

"Then how does he make money? How does he pay staff?" My eyes roll, she clearly thinks people are paying for sex.

"Guests can make donations, if they wish. There is a restaurant, and a bar, there are also small hotel style rooms that people can pay for to stay the night, but nobody sells sex, it's a safe place" Looking up she was staring at me.

"Roxy, was amazing, she was new and was exactly like me we both had our own fantasy, one that was the exact same, We didn't pay each other or the business for it" Georgina's gasp making me look at her, I don't understand why she is shocked.

"You have used the business? You actually did something in one of those places?" She is looking at me like she is disgusted, I need to figure out what to say next, this isn't going to plan at all.

"No, I didn't. Not exactly, there are rooms with the windows in yes, so workers can make sure everyone is okay, if something isn't consented or if someone is distressed the workers can see. Everything is mutual, I didn't do anything in a room with a window, I used Jackson's room, it was a fun night,

we sat drinking and laughing, sorry not night, day"
She is still looking at me like this is all wrong, I now
understand why he doesn't tell people about it,
people judge too quickly and are too closed minded
for these things. Jackson and Liam walked back into
the room, Liam looking happy.

"Well, now that's sorted what's the plan for Jacks
birthday?" He laughed seeming happy with what he
has been told, if only it was that simple for Georgina
"How the hell is it sorted? How is it even right, he
took Alena there to be used" Georgina is fuming, it
is clear she isn't going to let it pass, and I was hardly
used, she has taken the whole business wrong.

"Georgina, wind down. Seriously, it was fine, it's
legit, I doubt she was kicking and screaming" Liam
looking at her smiling.

"Okay, maybe she was but in a good way" Liam is
asking for a slap, I can see her anger growing, the
fact she doesn't understand it.

"Whatever, if I don't agree with it, I don't have to"
She was sulking, outnumbered and sulking, I know
though with time she will come around to the idea.

"I think something quiet is best" Jackson pointed
out, I have to agree, I don't think I can handle much
excitement right now.

"You said there's a restaurant and bar at the place,
right? Let's go and see exactly what it's like" Liam's
suggesting not exactly the best, I feel he is saying it
to annoy Georgina, and to annoy Jackson as I know
he hates the idea of Liam going there.

"I don't think so, that isn't a good idea, and I can't just take people on a tour, so they can have a peek, seriously only the people seriously interested in using it can be shown around" Jackson looked as shocked as me, and his answer a strong no.

No, let's go, I want to see exactly what this place is like, I want to see if it's as bad as I think" Everyone turned to Georgina, is she for real? She is the last person I would expect to say let's go there, yet here she is saying it is a good idea, I don't think it is, and Jackson doesn't seem sure either.

"Come on Jackson, we'll be on our best behavior, At least this way Georgina can see it's not as bad as she thinks, and there aren't people dangling from the ceilings, crying and being whipped" Laughter escapes my mouth hearing Liam's words, not the best thing for him to say considering there is a chance there will be, it is BDSM what do they expect to see?

"Okay, I will call through and make sure there is a table for four available" Jackson stood there shaking his head, not believing he was agreeing.

"Five" I smile looking at him.

"Why five?" He is looking at me confused, Georgina and Liam are as well.

"Well, because you didn't tell me it was your birthday, I have already text Roxy and invited her round for a catch up, she should be here soon" I can't help but smile, especially at Georgina's shocked face, Jackson looks rather pleased though and Liam as always looking at me confused.

"Five it is then" Jackson walked off, holding the phone to his ear, he walked into his office, a couple of seconds later he emerged.

"Sorted, there is a table being reserved for us, we will wait for Roxy then set off, Liam and Georgina you go together, me, Alena and Roxy will go together" Sitting no one said anything, everyone quiet waiting for Roxy to come, Georgina is clearly preparing herself for what she was about to see. To be honest, I have no idea how tonight will plan out, can we trust Georgina not to judge the guests while there, and can we trust Liam not to try sneak up to the rooms, one thing I know for sure, Jackson has his work cut out tonight. Roxy showing up, we invited her in, she looks around confused at Georgina and Liam been here.

"We are going out, to Jacksons work for his birthday" Smiling at her, I explain the change of plan she nods staying quiet, clearly feeling off with Liam and Georgina stood looking at her, Georgina needs to behave.

"Liam and Georgina are going in their car, you can come with us if you like?" Looking at her waiting she nods in agreement, us all leaving getting in our cars. Driving we don't speak much, it feels weird us been in the car together, slowly pulling up to Seductive Vibrations I can't help but smile, this place is truly amazing.

5 THREE IS NOT A CROWD

Walking in, Georgina is in amazement, looking around.

"It's beautiful, and everyone is dressed" I can't hold in my laughter at her comment about people being dressed, she seriously looks surprised.

"Mr. Reeves, It's great to see you, your table is this way" The young woman guided us to our table, leaving us with menus before walking off.

"Why did she call you Mr. Reeves? Our name is Woodcock, not Reeves" Liam is looking at him confused, Jackson shook his head, warning him to not say anything. I remember he told me about it, he doesn't use his real name, so people wouldn't contact him outside of work, so I didn't even think to question it. He has done it, so his outside life doesn't conflict with work life and vice versa. Sitting down, we ate, everyone laughing even Georgina was pleasant, especially towards Roxy which is a relief, finishing eating we moved to the bar.

"So, it isn't as bad as I thought, I will be honest, it is actually really nice down here" Georgina smiles, she has drunk way too much, but at least she is not shouting that it is a brothel or something worse. It is getting late, guests coming and going.

"Okay, we better go get a taxi, none of us can drive in this state" Georgina is laughing, almost falling off her chair, I can't believe just how wasted she is, considering she thought this place was awful, she has relaxed a lot.

"No need to call a taxi, I told the staff to keep three rooms free for us, so you can all have your own room" Jackson informed her, her face shocked.

"I am not sleeping here, with windows and people looking" She is gone, way too far gone, why did we let her drink so much, like we could actually control her or stop her drinking so much.

"No Georgina, not in that sort of room, the little hotel room, with a lock, and windows to outside, with curtains" I can't help but laugh at Jackson's tone, like she is a child that needs it explaining to her. Liam is smiling, he looks way to happy about this arrangement, Jackson noticing quickly squashing his hopes.

"Not a chance Liam, you're sleeping down here, not

upstairs" I can't help snickering to myself at Liam's disappointment from Jacksons words.

"I will show these two to their rooms, I will leave you two to catch up" Jackson points out, smiling at me and Roxy, he walks to the desk, getting the woman's attention behind it and the security.

"Take a good look at him, under no circumstances is he allowed upstairs, make sure everyone on duty knows as well" I can't control myself, howling with laughter Roxy looking at me like I have lost the plot.

"I was worried, you took so long replying, I thought I'd done something wrong, or that you didn't enjoy yourself with me" Roxy's voice soft, her eyes focusing on me, I had a lot of texts from her, but I just didn't reply because of what happened with Caroline.

"No, don't be daft, thing's happened that totally messed things up for me, I was bed bound for a few weeks" I smiled, and she grinned at me cheekily.

"I wish I meant that type of bound" I begin laughing realising what she meant, I didn't mean sexually.

"So, you weren't avoiding me because I said that I thought Jackson was fit? I honestly thought you were trying to keep away from me because of it, I thought you saw me as a threat, although I'm not sure why" Her voice quiet, why would I see her as a threat? She is so genuine and kind, and now knowing what Caroline looks like, I know she isn't his type. He certainly has a thing for redheads.

"Look, as long as you're not going to try and kill me

to get me out the way, I have no issues at all"
Smiling, I have to admit, her crushing on Jackson is
totally fine with me, she moved forward, her mouth
coming towards mine, trying to kiss me, I move
back, I don't feel comfortable doing this.

"I am not sure that's a good idea, I don't know what
Jackson will say or think" I apologise, I have to I
wouldn't like being turned down, I have to admit,
me and Jackson have not even discussed this part of
our relationship, I don't know if I'd be okay with him
going and sleeping with other women. I was willing
to give this up, my fantasy and everything and never
live it again if it mean Jackson didn't sleep with
other women. Jackson walked over sitting down.

"I can see me not sleeping tonight" He laughed, my
eyes widening with shock.

"Not that way, I meant I have a feeling Liam is going
to try causing trouble, I can just sense it" He
laughed at me and my reaction what else was I
meant to think he meant.

"Anyway, what are you two talking about?" He
moved back getting comfy smiling, I begin to shake
my head ready to say nothing important, but Roxy
begins to laugh.

"I tried to kiss her, she moved back because of you"
Wow, she is honest, I would be blushing with
embarrassment if I was her, Jackson turned to look
at me, confusion on his face.

"Let's walk outside for a minute, we'll be right back
Roxy" He grabs my hand, pulling me up, he leads me

outside, walking for a minute, he stops, his eyes staring into mine, his arms grabbing me, pulling my body to his, kissing me passionately, a demanding kiss, I love it.

"What do you want Alena? What do you want from me, what do you expect from me?" His eyes looking deep into mine, sending me into overdrive. Why is he asking what I want and expect from him, I want to be happy with him and him be happy with me, simple.

"I want you, I want you to feel safe like I do, I do want more yes, but I don't want you to move on" I don't even know if that makes sense to me let alone him, I just don't feel comfortable saying that I would like to sleep with Roxy again.

"If you want more, and Roxy is your more, you can have it, I won't stop you, why do you think I'd move on?" His lips push against mine, his body pushing me back against a wall, my breathing getting faster, my hands grasping his hair, I need him now.

"Well, I am waiting" His eyes looking at me, right now really? Can't this conversation wait till a bit later?

"Because if I sleep with Roxy, that then means you can sleep with others as well, I don't want that sort of relationship" He smiled, his body pushing against mine harder, his lips connecting with mine, moaning I pull him to me, wanting more of him.

"You can have anything you want, but all I want is you, I want to see you happy, see you fulfilled in every way possible, if you want me to join in sometimes, then that's fine, if not then that is fine, I only need you. I don't plan on walking in there or anywhere and finding someone else to sleep with just because you and Roxy sleep together" His kissing pushing me over the edge, my arms, trying to unfasten his buttons, moaning against his lips, his hands wrapping around me lifting me, moving my legs I wrap them around him moaning, feeling his shaft pushing against my sex.

"I just want to give you what you need Alena, I have everything I want with you" Looking at him, I can't control myself, moaning my hands begin to unfasten his trousers.

"Right now, I need you" His arms wrapping around me, his lips kissing my neck.

"Outside really?" His voice against my neck, making me moan.

"Yes, but only because I know the gate that leads round here is locked and needs a code, so no one is coming around here, just fuck me" My hands grasping his hair, his hands sliding my skirt up, his hands pulling my thong off, ripping it. Moaning from the pleasure, my hands pull his trousers down, moaning I grasp his cock, his hands grabbing mine, pinning them above my head with one hand, his other hand pushing is cock against my pussy.

"Fuck, I missed my pussy" His hips thrust quick, my screams loud as his hips moved quick, no escape for me, I don't want to, moaning, I feel the orgasm rising, I need more of him, I need him to push me to my limits. His hips moving faster and harder, moaning, I pull him to me, his hand grasping my throat I love it when he does it, my body screaming, his cock pounding into me, the orgasm rocketing around my body, my mind running away, his hand, grasping my chin, his eyes looking in mine, watching as the orgasm took my control away, his hips slowing before he pulled away. His lips pressing on mine.

"Come on, you must be shattered, let's get in and get settled for the night" I do feel exhausted, my mind is tired, my body ready to collapse, sorting myself out, I lean on him, walking back inside, we go to Roxy.

"Are you guys okay?" She is looking at me confused, we have been gone a while.

"We've never been better, other than being ready to crash out any second, but yeah we're great" I smile at her, my eyes feeling heavy.

"Okay, well, I'll catch up with you tomorrow, I'm off to bed myself, see you in the morning" Watching as she walks off, we head up to our room. Walking in my body slumps on the bed, I am exhausted.

"I'm surprised you didn't invite her back up here" Jackson looked at me confused, I would love to but there's not a chance I can do that now. He is looking at me wondering why I am not replying, instead of just asking like he always does, he climbs on top of me, he's looking at me laughing, his hands tickling me, I hate being tickled, screaming I try to escape.

"What's wrong with you? I've seen you after, you loved it so why not, I told you I won't go with anyone else, so there is no need to worry" His hand, lifting my top up, so he can continue the tickle torture on my bare skin, my hands pulling it right back down, I squirm moving away, his eyes on mine.

"What's wrong? Alena, this isn't like you, by now you'd usually be helping me take your top off, not pulling it back on" His question making me realise he wasn't stupid or fooled, looking at him I have to be honest.

"It's hideous" I mutter quiet, the thought of the scar in my mind.

"What hideous?" His eyes looking at me confused, then something clicked, and his expression changed his eyes understanding.

"Alena, your scar is far from Hideous, are you afraid of people seeing it, of me seeing it? Is this why you lifted the blanket to cover yourself today, you never pull a blanket over" His eyes looking into mine, he looks like he has to try fix me, all I can do is nod a reply. His eyes realising I meant it.

"Right, stop there, don't move" He grabbed his phone, lifting up my top, I was about to pull it back down, his eyes looking into mine, I stop myself, watching as he took a picture of my scar, he was doing something on the phone, then he turned it to show me, wow I can't help but look at it in disgust.

"What do you see?" His question causing a tear to roll down my cheek.

"I see something horrible, that people will look at in disgust" I do, it is not appealing at all, if I can't look at without disgust and it is on my body how will anyone else?   The scars Max left where small, nothing like this.

"Okay, what about this one? Would you be happy if your scar looked more like this?" He turned the phone, looking at this one, compared to mine, yes, I would, it isn't as bad as mine.

"Anything looks better than that, but yes, that looks better than mine" I admit, it does, how is this meant to help?   Turning the phone, he shows me yet another picture.

"What do you think of this one?" Looking at it, I take the picture in.

"It doesn't look too bad, but what's the point in this, to show me how scars look?" I am confused, totally confused.

"The point is, the second picture I showed you is your scar, I showed you a bad one first, so you would realise your scar is nothing, and is not as bad as you see it to be" Looking down at my scar, it looks so different before it didn't look like this, my mind playing tricks on me, it really isn't as bad as I thought it was, lying next to me his arms wrapping around me, cuddling me tightly as I fell asleep against him. Waking up, opening my eyes Jackson lying with his eyes closed, looking at him, I can't help but wonder how I managed to get him, he was in Georgina's league not mine, yet he chose me. I think back to Jessica, or rather Caroline, and how similar we are, he clearly has a thing for redheads, that's for sure. Slowly sliding out of bed, I head out into the hall, grabbing some food I sit and eat, the place quiet, finishing, I walked back in, Jackson still asleep on the bed, climbing onto the bed, my legs on either side of him, leaning down I kiss his lips softly, beckoning him to wake up. His eyes open, looking at me, I begin to move, my kisses running down to his neck, I need him again, my lips trailing down to his chest, kissing his torso as I keep going. My mouth finally reaching his groin, I plan to be very sinful, glancing up at him, smiling, I pull down his pants, exposing his velvet shaft, with my hand I slowly caress it, my hand moving up and down slowly, feeling him become hard in my hand. Slowly I begin lowering my head towards the tip, my tongue gently gliding over the tip of him, my eyes watching as his expression changes, he tastes ripe, it makes me want more, my fingers keep caressing his cock up and down, while my other hand finds his balls, grabbing them tightly, I plan to draw this out for as long as possible, to give him as much pleasure as I can. My hand begins to move faster, teasing and taunting, my mouth, sucking the end of his cock in, my own moans growing from the taste, my hand gripping harder, moving, working it up and down, exposing his head as I do, my tongue trailing down the length of his cock then back up again. Reaching the top my tongue flicking it before, I suck him into my mouth. His fingers finding my hair as he grabs it, my mouth lowering more, taking more of him inside me. His hand tugs on my hair, a groan escaping my mouth from the feel, I can feel my lips vibrating against his cock when I groan, moving to position myself, I sucked most of him inside me, sliding his cock in and out of my mouth at a good speed. My hand grasping his balls tighter, my tongue rubbing against him as I move and when I reach the end, my tongue darting over it quickly, his breathing becoming rapid, I love it, his groans growing in intensity, my tongue swiveling around his cock while it is inside my mouth. I want to taste every inch of him, I keep moving my head, so his cock can slide in and out while my hands tease, his grip becoming tighter on my hair as I get him closer to the edge, closer to surrendering himself to me, my own arousal awakening, my eyes watching his face, the sound of him moaning with pleasure sending me wild. His hands grasping my hair harder, holding my head in place, his hips thrusting, his cock is moving faster in and out of my mouth, my tongue keeps swirling, my grip getting tightener around his balls, his cock pushing into my mouth, sliding down my throat gagging me slightly, the feel of it pulsing in my mouth as his hips jerked, his hot cum running down my throat. Starting to pull away, there is a knock at the door, he is going to ignore it, you can clearly see. Shaking his head, he realises he can't if it is Liam he can't have him wandering around here. He climbed off the bed, walking towards the door, climbing into the bed, I cover myself up, Jackson walks back through with Roxy in tow, she sat down on the bed and looked at me.

"I'm interrupting something, aren't I? I just came to see, well it doesn't matter, it can wait" She moved, getting ready to walk out, taking the plunge I stop her.

"No, you're not, why don't you stay and join us?" What am I doing? She is looking at me and then at Jackson, Jackson looks like he wasn't sure what to do now, I don't know either, but I know I am hot, ravenous and I want more, pulling her to me, I start to kiss her, her body going into shock than her lips started kissing me back. She is climbing onto the bed, her legs straddling me, her hands pulling my shirt off, I can see Jackson out the corner of my eye ready to leave, he clearly thinks he isn't invited.

"Don't leave, come here" her lips starting kissing down my neck, Jackson looking at her, he clearly won't without her approval.

"Roxy are you okay with Jackson joining?" My voice quiet as I wait, her lips kissing me more, my mind exploding fuck I want her, what am I doing, did I really just invite Jackson to play with me and another woman? Will I feel guilty if he touches her?

"I am happy for him to join yes" her lips began kissing me again, my moans getting louder, Jackson walking over, climbing on the bed, his lips pressing against mine as hers keep moving down, it feels unusual, I can feel her lips getting closer to my core, his hands grasping my breasts. Her lips finally reaching my pool of moisture, she is slowly stimulating it with her tongue, Jacksons mouth kissing my breasts, my body being teased from all angels, and every inch of me is burning with pleasure. Gazing down at them, both deep into enjoying the taste of my body, Jackson moved, grabbing the blindfold, he places it over my eyes, his hands grasping mine, tying them above my head. I can feel them both moving, lips kissing mine, Roxy's lips, I can recognise them instantly, she tastes so sweet, my body jumps, something like glass sliding across my nipple, the coldness trailing down my body, rubbing over my clit, it reaches my sex, the glass rubbing gently, then it plunges inside of me, I have lost control, the feeling is insane, I can feel the cold glass as Roxy's kisses move down to my neck, Jackson's warm tongue starting to lick around the glass, a combination of cold and warm setting of fireworks in my body, moaning loud, my hands want to grasp Jacksons hair. Roxy's hand gripping my breasts, her mouth, sucking them in slowly, her tongue teasing them, twirling around the peak with circular motions. It is like I am being seduced, and I really don't want it to stop, my body jumps, screams escape my mouth, a sharp snap across my stomach, my pussy getting instantly wetter as the leather hits my skin. The glass starts to move, slowly in and out, moaning from the pleasure, it builds up speed, the whip hitting again making me moan. All the different sensations are driving me crazy, I want to touch, to play, instead I lay here while their seduction continues. My breathing slow and relaxed, my mind feels free, there is nothing in it now, except this moment and my pleasure. Roxy's mouth keeps teasing my breasts, Jackson's tongue flicking against my clit, the glass, swirling around and pumping in and out of me.

"Is this what you wanted?" Jackson asked his breath touching my clit, my scream loud, another sharp whip hitting across my breasts, moaning in delight, begging for more, they keep going. Building up the speed, working together to set me free from the orgasm building inside me, my whole body shaking with pleasure as I reached my destination, my orgasm taking over, Jacksons hands removing the blindfold, his hands untying mine, he moved, settling between my legs, his arms spreading them wider, pulling me to him. My hands trailed down Roxy's neck, sliding over her breasts, grasping them gently, I continue to move down, my fingers finding her soft sweet opening. My fingers rubbing gently against her sex, her juices running freely over my fingers. Jackson's cock probing my entrance, teasing me a little before he pulled back out, slowly pushing the tip in again and withdrawing himself watching as I moan, pushing my pussy up trying to get more, Roxy's mouth teasing my breasts, her teeth gently biting down, my fingers slowly sliding inside of her, rubbing around, she is so warm and moist. Jackson still teasing me with his tip, my hand grabs the glass dildo, running it down Roxy's body watching her squirm, Jacksons eyes on me, his pleasure rising seeing me enjoying myself. Tugging on my nipples, I push the dildo inside her making her moan against my skin. My hand, turning it slightly, moving it in and out building up a rhythm, Jackson stopped teasing me, his hands grasping my hips, my mind, getting ready for his thrust, he pushed hard and deep inside me, a scream escaping my mouth as he did, he pulled himself out again, my body shaking, no, he can't do this to me. He keeps taunting me, his cock plunging inside me hard and fast, my screams loud, just to pull himself out again, my body trying to move further down, closer to him, but it is useless his grip is tight, holding me firmly in place. My hand moves faster, the toy making Roxy moan, her mouth against my breasts, her juices running over my fingers. Jacksons hand grabbed another toy, smiling at me, his hand rubbing around my butt, panic in eyes, and he smiled realising.

"Relax, you said you trust me" I do, I need to relax, my mind concentrating on Roxy rather than the toy he was about to push into my arse. My hand moving the toy faster, the pleasure on Roxy's face growing. Jacksons hand pushing the toy inside me, the vibrations through my ass making me moan, my hand struggling to move the toy that is in Roxy. Jackson's hard thrust drove his cock deep into my pussy, my screams loud enough for everyone to hear, ready for him to pull back out, he didn't his hips started moving slowly, my moans growing, my hand pushing the dildo in and out of Roxy faster and harder, her lips kissing my breasts. The sensation from Jackson thrusting his cock inside me and the vibrations in my butt has my mind spiraling out of control, I am being greedy, but I still want more. My hand begins to move the glass dildo faster, harder ensuring it twisted each time it came out, I am struggling to keep going, my own pleasure building up, Jackson is pounding faster and harder, my screams getting louder. Roxy placing her hand over my mouth to muffle my screams. Jackson grabs something from next to the bed, he threw it at Roxy, she slid the ball into my mouth, her hand grasping my breasts, my screams muffled by the gag. Moving the dildo I can see Roxy getting closer, Jacksons, hand rising, his hand closing around my neck, his hips thrusting harder and deeper inside of me, his hand grasping in Roxy's hair, the faster and harder he goes the more I can feel the vibrations, I can feel them all over my body, I can't take much more, I let myself go, giving myself up to him, my pussy pulsates and worshipping his cock as I exploded, every part of me shaking, lightning bolts rippling through my body, his hands flipped me over, pulling me onto my knees, my hands on the bed. His cock pushing inside of me again, a whimper escaping my lips, Roxy moves in front of me, moving my head up to align with her pussy, I slide the dildo in again, my body moving with every thrust from Jackson, his hands gripping my waist, holding me in place, my hand moves the glass faster and harder, my tongue licking her clit, my mouth sucking on it gently, she tastes amazing. Her hand grasps my hair, holding my mouth against her clit, Jacksons hands grasping my neck, pulling it hard, moaning I feel myself build back up, my hand working harder and faster watching as Roxy finally gave in to her orgasm, her screams loud, her body pushing down on the dildo, forcing my mouth to take more of her, my own moans mirroring hers as another orgasm explodes inside of me, collapsing next to next other on the bed, Jackson pulls the toy out of my ass, lying here we don't speak, just trying to regulate our breathing again. A while later, Jackson's phone rang, he answers it listening to what is being said, but not talking.

"I will be right down" I look at him, wondering what was happening.

"Liam is trying to get upstairs, we need to get dressed and go down" All three of us getting dressed, we walk downstairs, sure enough there is Liam being held back by two men.

"Seriously, you can't trust me to walk to your room?" He looks rather frustrated that he couldn't get upstairs.

"Look Liam, if you want to use the services here you can, but you'll have to book in and follow the rules like everyone else" Jackson looked at the receptionist.

"What like she does? So, it's okay to bend the rules for her?" Liam is clearly not happy, his finger pointing at me.

"Liam, she is my partner, so yes, she can use this building just like me" Jackson says it softly, trying to not cause more trouble as guests are watching.

"Shut it Liam, you're only pissed because you tried it on with me last night and I pushed you away" Georgina laughs at him. Wow, he must have grown some balls to try it on with Georgina, I can't help but laugh, Jackson joins in as well, Liam looks ashamed.

"Let's just go, this isn't the place" Jackson starts walking towards the exit, Jackson turns throwing his keys at me, catching them, I look at him with pure shock on my face, is actually letting me drive his car?

"You trust me with your car?" Looking at him like he is crazy I have to ask.

"Well, you trust me with your life so why not, plus you can ride well enough in the bedroom so let's see how you can handle my baby" His tone cocky, Georgina laughing as she walked passed getting in the car with Liam. Climbing in it feels so nice, he might just regret this. Starting the engine, the car roars to life, the sounds, making me moan, it sounds amazing. Putting it in gear I speed out of the car park, Jackson in the passenger seat, Roxy in the back, It is so smooth and easy to use, I feel the speed building as I go faster, looking in the mirror, I can see Liam behind us in his car, I can't help but smile, the rush is amazing, Jacksons hand starting to rub down my leg and back up, finally settling between them.

"Are you trying to make me crash"? I laugh trying to keep my eyes on the road.

"Nope, I just want to see how much you can take before you tell me to stop because you're going to crash" Jackson's reply like a challenge, he wants to see how far he can take me while I drive. I am not sure I like this game he is playing, he is clearly teasing and taunting me for his own amusement, but I love it. His hand lifting my skirt up, then slowly pulling my thong down, his hand moving up to my breasts, slowly stroking them under my shirt, I am already losing concentrating, his hand suddenly moving down my stomach, stroking gently before sliding into my trousers. Trying my hardest to concentrate on the road, I am not that easy I don't give up that quick, but I am finding it harder, to be honest, it is becoming a lot harder to concentrate, his fingers started to slide into my pussy.

"I seem to be winning, you have slowed down" Jackson's voice is playful, his fingers moving faster, my eyes looking up to the dial, he is right I have slowed right down. Pushing my foot on the pedal, I begin to speed back up, Jackson telling me Roxy's address, I need to either concentrate or quit, I need to get Roxy home safely, Jacksons fingers moving even faster, my breathing getting heavier.

"If only we could get Roxy in the front as well" Jackson voice full of humour, his fingers still going, moving in and out of my pussy, my breathing getting faster, my mind trying to concentrate on the road, Roxy sitting watching in amazement, waiting for me to tell him to stop, I am determined to get her home before I quit. My body jumps from the shock, something warm and moist against my neck, looking in the mirror, sure enough Roxy has joined in, her mouth kissing my neck, I can't deal with them both teasing together and still concentrate on driving.

"This is cheating, I can't believe you would help him win Roxy" I am actually gutted she has, she should be helping me not distracting me more.

"Any reason to kiss your neck and I am game" She laughs. Roxy's house is literally two streets away, just two, her mouth teasing more, Jackson's fingers moving faster, moaning I stop the car.

"Looks like I win" Panting, I look outside at Roxy's house.

"Apparently so, she has won Jackson, I did wonder how far you'd get with all of this happening though" Roxy laughs climbing out the car.

"Shall I help you finish?" Jackson's voice, matching is cunning smile, is he joking, he has to be joking!

"No!" I refuse, although I want him to, I have to refuse. Saying goodbye to Roxy, I begin driving, Jackson finally behaving, two minutes down the road his fingers starting to play, of course he wouldn't listen to me. Looking around I take a turn into a field, driving down a bit, I switch the engine off.

"What are you doing?" Jackson's eye son me, as I begin sliding down my trousers.

"Getting what is mine" Looking at him, I climb on top of him, kissing him full force. My hands working on removing his cock from his trousers, Slowly I lower my pussy down on his cock, my hips instantly bucking, moaning feeling him inside me. I can feel his shaft moving in and out of me, his lips kissing my neck, in between kisses his teeth nibbling making me moan.

"You don't get what you want, you get what I give" His voice a growl, his hands gripping my waist, holding me still, his hips beginning to thrust hard, pounding his cock inside me, my hands grasping his hair. His hands release me, grasping one of my hands, he grabs the rope, his hand tying mine to my ankle, then the same with the other side. Both my hands now tied to my ankles, his smile wicked, his hand grasping my hair.

"You get what I give, nothing more" His hands gripping my waist again, his hips moving fast and hard, moaning from pleasure, I wish I could touch him. I need more, I want so much more, this is amazing, but I can't stop thinking I want more. One of his hands moving, grasping my hair, he begins pulling it harder, my screams getting louder as his hips thrust quicker, pushing me to my limit and over instantly, moaning I collapse against him, panting on top of him, I have no idea how this happened, his hands beginning to untie my ankles and wrists, lifting me, he slides over into the driver's seat.

"Good call, I don't think I could drive home right now" Laughing, my body shaking from the pleasure.

"What did you mean by wanting more? You said it during sex" Looking at me intrigued, I didn't realise I had said it out loud, I thought it was in my head, shrugging my shoulders at him I answer.

"If I knew what I wanted more of, I would have found it by now" Confessing to him, I just know each time we have sex, or do anything sexual I feel the need for more, I could be tied up, blindfolded yet I still feel I want more. I wonder if it is even possible, I am sure of one thing though, if anyone can give me the more I am wanting, it is Jackson, no one else, just Jackson. Arriving back at his, he starts cooking, looking at him, I am in awe I cannot cook, not at all.

"I never see you cooking why?" He looks at me, while mixing the food.

"I can't cook, we live on takeaways, restaurants and well ready meals" I can't help but laugh at it, me, Georgina and Liam cannot cook, yet Jackson is here, like a chef, how is that even possible. His eyes looking up at me, he looks shocked.

"Seriously?" Yes, he certainly is in shock.

"Really, none of us can cook, so we just got used to eating what others cook and deliver" It really isn't a big deal, yet he looks astounded by the thought.

"You can't live like that, seriously at some point you will need to learn to cook, you can't exactly be healthy eating that junk" He begins opening cupboards, serving up the food, he put it on the plates, carrying them to the table. Sitting we ate, his eyes on me the whole time.

"Are you sure you're okay with tomorrow?" Looking up at Jackson, I can't say I am, but I also can't say I'm not.

"I can't say I am but I am also not, it just feels weird going to the grave, I never knew Katie, but I am happy to go and support you, I know tomorrow will be hard, so I will be here in any way you need me to be, plus I am not sure your mum will even like me" Laughing at the thought, what if his mum doesn't like me? I am going to be the one feeling uncomfortable then, stood at her daughter's grave.

"Thank you, I just want you by my side that is all, my mum will love you, I know she will" He is so sweet, something tells me he is saying that because his mum loved Caroline, and in a way, I am like her.

"Bedtime come on" His hand gripping mine, walking upstairs together, climbing into bed, Jackson falling asleep, lying here my mind on tomorrow, on his mum, his sister, I am scared if I am honest, I don't know her other than from how Liam has described her throughout the years, he has said she can be mean quite a lot. Kissing Jackson on the head, whispering Goodnight to him, I nuzzle into him, falling asleep instantly. Waking I roll over, Jackson still asleep, looking at him, I should really try cooking breakfast for a change, it can't be that hard surely? Climbing out of bed, walking downstairs quietly I start cooking, the plan is eggs, bacon and everything if I can. The egg turns into a disaster, throwing them in the bin, sausage and bacon just didn't go well at all, putting toast in the toaster I switch it on, this I can cook. Jackson walking down the stairs looking intrigued.

"Your cooking?" He looks across at me, humour on his face as he looks at the mess I have made.

"Failing, so here, have some toast" Walking over I put the plate down, sitting he eats it, at least I could make toast.

"So, why do you never seem to be at work?" I am interested, he seems to always be away from it.

"I don't need to be, I have a lot of people there, it runs smoothly every now and then I go in for meetings, I get calls about issues, but mostly the managers do a good enough job" Nodding I understand what he means.

"You have to think, sometimes I was away for nearly a year on missions, they had to deal without me, so they tend to do it even when I am here, sure every now and then they ask me to go in, but they run the place by my rules" It is good how he can leave and know the businesses will be safe.

"So, you haven't said about the navy yet, what is happening with it?" I need to know if it is something he is still doing, I would like to know now rather than just being told later.

"The navy is like a home to me, I have friends, they are more than friends, they are my brothers who I usually do missions with Marcus is one of the closest ones, he is currently on a mission with the rest of the team, I might get called in, but highly unlikely, I don't actually plan to go back on missions, or sign up for longer" I am glad, the thought of him going back and possibly losing him is scary.

"Okay, so who are the guys you usually go on missions with?" I don't even know if he can tell me that, I just want to know more about him, more about his life, because I don't really know much about it.

"Well, Marcus, Troy, Alexander and Joel are the four main guys, we have each other's backs. A few times we have needed support we have been there, we are like brothers, we will fight for each other and take a bullet for each other. To be honest, I miss them, being back here, I don't see them often, Marcus and everyone lives close, but they have their own lives" He clearly cares about them, a lot I can see just by the way he is talking about them, there is so much respect and love there.

"You said you have two businesses? What is the other, I just noticed you never told me" He is smiling at me, okay, so now I am intrigued with the look on his face.

"Remind me another time, Liam is here" He stood up walking to the door, opening it, sure enough Liam walks in.

"Ready?" Liam stood looking at us both.

"Of course, you're usually the late one, we're meeting mum there" Jackson grabbing his jacket looking at me, well this is it, if I don't puke on the way it will be amazing. Walking outside, we get in the car, this feels weird, and well, awkward, please hurry up and get us there, my mind reminding me of the last time there was three of us in the car, me, Roxy and Jackson, my mind replaying what happened, now there is three but instead of Roxy it is Liam and it feels wrong. Arriving at the graveyard, I can't help but feel relief, Liam leading the way, Jackson holding my hand us walking behind. The woman at the grave looks old, like she has aged far quicker than she should have. She walked towards us, her arms wrapping around me, a smile on her face. "Hi Alena, I'm Helen, Jackson's mum. You look well all things considered" She is smiling, hugging me tight, she seems nice, Liam had her sound scary and mean.

"Hi mum" Jackson smiled, she let go of me, hugging him, Jackson kissing her cheek, walking to the grave they laid flowers, reminiscing and discussing what has happened recently. I feel out of place, like I shouldn't be here, I have no idea who Katie was, and I never met her. Her grave reflects someone who is loved dearly though, next to it lay's Jackson's daughter, her grave equally as beautiful. I said I would come to support Jackson, and I am, I can't ignore the awkward feeling of being here, but I can support Jackson. Walking out, Jackson is walking with Liam, me and Helen walking behind.

"Thank you, for what you did for Liam, not many would do that" She smiled, her eyes showing her pain, I can't imagine how she feels losing Katie, and I am sure knowing Liam was missing for those days was just as bad.

"I am glad I did, I couldn't just leave him in possible danger, he is a very good friend of mine" Smiling he is, Liam is a good friend.

"Well, either way thank you, even if Caroline said she wouldn't hurt him, I am grateful, I don't think I can take losing another child, I will be forever grateful" She smiled, we reached the cars.

"Liam, you are coming home with me, I need your help. Alena it was lovely meeting you, hopefully I see you again soon" She hugged Jackson and climbed into her car, Liam joining her, I can't help but feel sorry for her, for her heartache and the disaster she has had to go through with Katie and then with Liam as well. Climbing into the car Jackson started the engine, smiling I look at him.

"So, the second business, what is it?" I am curious, and I want to know.

"You have already seen it sort of" How have I

already seen it? What have I missed?

"Okay, well you can explain because I have no idea what you're talking about" What is it?

"In Seductive Vibrations, there's a shop. I also have standalone shops" His explanation not helping much, oh no I realise, okay, sex shop, what else was I expecting it is obvious if it is connected to Seductive Vibrations. The name is so easy for me to say now, it just rolls off my tongue freely, I feel like if anyone asked about it, I won't be embarrassed anymore, arriving back at his we walk in quietly, I don't understand how he got into all this, all the BDSM and the business, he doesn't look abused or broken, sure he is heartbroken but that was clearly after he was involved in it. Arriving at his we walk into the house, his eyes watching me.

"What are you thinking Alena? You have that look where you are considering something?" Jacksons voice quiet.

"You seem so normal, not damaged, it is confusing, I assumed most people into this sort of stuff were damaged" It sounds bad now I have said it out loud, but I am curious, a lot of people have said that to me as well. Something I remember being discussed in university and everyone had the opinion that it was a fact people who enjoy BDSM are damaged.

"It is a common misconception, just because we like things differently does not mean we are damaged. In fact, most of us are perfectly sound minded" Nodding to him he moves closer to me.

"How did you get into it? I mean, how did you figure out you liked it all?" I am interested in knowing, and then hopefully I can find out more about what he likes, really likes.

"I was eighteen, it was actually Marcus, who introduced me to the lifestyle, he had a brat, that is how I became interested, I just grew from there really, slowly learning and finding what I like, but also how to read a woman's body language" He moved, his body reaching mine, grabbing me.

"You said you wanted more, do you still have no idea how much more?" Looking at him, shaking my head in confusion, I wish it was easy to answer.

"Okay, well, why do you think you want or need more?" His voice seductive.

"I don't know, just no matter what you have done, I've enjoyed it, but I always feel like something is missing, like there should be more to come after, like I aren't getting everything, and I aren't getting all of you" That is the best way I can explain it, I can't figure it out myself. He looks at me like he understands, grabbing my hand, he walks upstairs, me following, heart racing, stopping at a room he turns facing me.

"Do you trust me?" Why keep asking this, laughing, I nod.

"I wouldn't be here if I didn't" I wouldn't if I didn't trust him I would not have been here the last few weeks, I would have been at home hiding.

"I am being serious Alena, do you trust me, and can

you keep an open mind?" Now he is worrying me, looking at him I wonder what is in this room, but to be honest, after what I have seen at Seductive Vibrations can it really be worse?

"I trust you yes, and I have an open mind, open enough to let you gag me" He put the code in, opening the door, walking in I feel speechless, it is not as bad as I expected, not at all, the room is small, it has whips, a bed, some sort of chair, what looks like a swing, just a mixture of things, to be honest one of the rooms in Seductive Vibrations looked more scary than this.

"Is this more?" His question seductive walking in, my hands feeling the items, I have no idea, how do I know if this is more? What I do know though is the thought of him having me in this room is making me wet.

"I don't know, how will I know if you don't check?" My tooth biting down on my lip, his arms wrapping around me.

"Strip" He demanded, turning I look at him in disbelief, is he being serious or is it a joke?

"You can either strip, or you can stand there fully clothes, but believe me, it'll feel much better without clothes on. Your other option is we walk out the room, any of the three is fine by me Alena, you can walk out anytime you want" His hand stroking my neck, I don't want to walk out this room, I don't want to miss what is going to happen, something tells me this is the more I am needing.

Moving away from him, I smile, my hands slowly removing the clothes, his eyes watching me, something about him being dominant makes me want to obey him, finally naked he pulls me towards the chair, my heart beginning to race, looking at him with fear and excitement in my eyes.

"This is the only time I will do it, I wouldn't be doing it now if you haven't gone on about needing more, so much during sex, this will be the only time Alena, after this, we need to talk, there are rules to this" His lips kissing mine, what rules come with this? I will agree to all the rules if he does it again, and I don't even know what is coming yet. Looking at the chair it is scary, there is no seat, he moved me, sitting me down, my body balancing on my legs and feet, his hands slowly tying my ankles and wrists to the chair, his mouth kissing down my neck slowly, reaching my breasts his lips kissing my nipples, then gently sucking them in his mouth, he keeps going, his mouth moving down, settling between my legs, his tongue teasing my wet pussy. His hands checking the straps are tight enough, my body already craving more of him, the leather straps making me moan.

"We will stick with red for now, red is your safe word Alena, later you can pick another, but right now, red is your safe word" His mouth starting kissing down my thigh, moaning I try push myself to him but it is useless. His mouth is sinful, moving slowly tasting me, slowly kissing back up my body, his lips pressing against mine, his hand gripping my hair and pulling my head back, his lips pressing against my exposed neck.

"You say the safeword when you have had enough, don't feel safe, or are overwhelmed and need me to stop. Not if your sulking and want your own way, you say it, I stop" Nodding I agree to his terms.

"Everything I use on you, I will tell you what it is, again, just this time, next time I won't" I need to ask what he means, I will but I will wait till after. He stood up, walking around his hands collecting items, a whip, a paddle, nipple clamps, along with other items I don't know about. His mouth kissing along my body again, reaching my neck, his teeth biting my ear, slowly kissing down my collar bone, keeping going he reaches my breasts, gently sucking on one.

"Ready?" He looks at me smiling, oh, I might regret this, but I have to see if it is, the more I want, nodding in response I feel the excitement flow through me.

6 MY HONEYPOT

He moved, his hand grabbing the paddle, gently hitting it across my breasts, yelping I jump from the pleasure, he followed the action on my other breast. Moving, his body kneeling between my legs, his mouth licking my breasts, his tongue trailing from one nipple to the other. His hand gripping one, the feel of the nipple clamp being attached, making me smile, his tongue trailing to the other nipple, his hand grasping the breast the feel of the nipple clamp being added to it. These are different, wires are attached, I can't help but wonder why there is wires. He moved, walking around the back, slowly running leather across my body, the whip making me moan, why do I enjoy the feel of leather so much? Standing behind me, his lips finding my neck, as soon as his lips kiss, the feel of electricity running through my breasts, making me jump, my heart pulsing faster, as the electric pulse stops, his mouth moving around kissing the back of my neck, an electric pulse shooting through my breasts again, moaning my teeth bite down on my lips, my pussy gathering moisture already. He keeps kissing, reaching my arm, his mouth slowly trailing kisses down reaching my hand, the leather whip swinging, hitting my inner thigh, jumping I scream, I want to grab him, I want to pull him to me, his mouth gently kissing where the whip has hit, lifting his head the whip swinging hitting the opposite side, my body jumping from the pleasure, his mouth kissing once again where the whip has hit. Standing up, the whip trailing along my body, his hand grabbing the blindfold, placing it over my eyes, my excitement increasing, I need him to touch me, to do something. His lips pressing against mine, moaning I go to pull him to me, my arms staying where they are, moving back, I can hear him, his movements, teasing screaming, I jump, the sharp sting across my left breast from where the whip has hit, he fell silent again, no movements, screaming, I jump, the whip hitting the right breast this time, I am trying not to scream, it is useless, I am enjoying it too much, I can't stop myself, I need to, I want to try and go as long as possible without showing him the full pleasure he is giving me. Staying quiet, I can't hear him, something cold touching my skin, jumping it runs along my shoulder, closing my eyes, feeling myself tense up with pleasure, the coldness moving down, leaving a trail of wet and coldness across my skin, slowly reaching my pubic bone, the cold runs between my legs, biting on my lip, stopping myself, I assume it is ice, he is holding it at my clit, making it freezing, slowing moving it again stopping at my pussy, his fingers pushing it inside me, screaming my try jump, the whip then hitting my breasts. I can't control myself, the coldness too much to handle, something warm now dripping across my collarbone, trailing down between my breasts, the warmth covering the cold making me moan, it is a good job I can't move because right now, I would be on him, he keeps going, the combination of hot and cold mixing making me moan louder, it's dripping onto my clit, gasping loud the whip swinging hitting my breasts, making me scream.

"Toy time" His voice quiet, the feel of glass sliding between my legs, it feels frozen, biting my lip I try to stop my screams, why is it so cold, it is like an ice cube, his hand plunging it inside me, crying loud as the whip hits again, jumping from the sensation I relax, he seems to whip me every time I make a noise, the dildo sitting inside me, it doesn't seem to be warming up, the feel of the whip trailing down my body reaching between my legs, the whip gently hitting my clit, biting down stopping my screams, if I scream I know there will be another whip, his chuckle quiet.

"You're learning" The whip hitting my skin harder,

forcing myself not to make a noise, the sound of him moving, the toy still frozen between my legs, sitting inside my pussy.

"Pinwheel" His voice quiet, coming from behind me, what is a pinwheel? Something cold touching my shoulder the feel of spikes, it's rolling across my skin, sliding over my breasts, moaning loud, I grasp the chair, it isn't hurting, while I can feel the pins pushing against my skin, it doesn't hurt the sensation is amazing, I can sense his body moving, stopping between my legs, kneeling between my legs, the pinwheel running across my body, reaching my leg, it keeps moving down, then rolling back up to my chest. Jumping at the feel of the toy pushing against my ass, slowly rubbing before he pushes it inside me, screaming in shock and pleasure, the whip hits my breasts, jumping screams escape my lips, his whip hitting again, my teeth clamping down on my lips, his hand begins moving the toy into the right position, turning it on, my body jumping from the vibrations shooting through me, the pinwheel moving over my leg again.

"Gag" His hand pushing it inside my mouth, fastening it in place, at least I can't scream now, that is a good thing. His hand pushing what feels like a ball into my hand.

"Your get out card, you can't say red so drop the ball if you want me to stop" My mind feels overwhelmed, my whole-body begging for him, begging for more, he seems to be keeping me right on the tipping point of an orgasm. His hand moving the toy in and out slowly, the glass still feeling frozen, moaning, suddenly his fingers pushing inside me next to the toy, the hot and cold together making me scream, I can't scream the gag muffling it. The sensations are sending me wild, my ass vibrating from the toy, I can feel my moisture dripping out of me, his mouth slowly kissing my clit, his tongue sneaking out and flicking the end of my clit. The pinwheel rolling along the inside of my legs, he is going slow, teasing purposely stopping me from finishing, my breathing perfectly relaxed how is that possible? My mind going crazy. I need a resolution to the pleasure, the orgasm building within me, my body relaxing, my mind feeling free, I feel free, I can't think of anything but the pleasure right here and now, nothing else matters. I feel like I have, the more I needed, his hand beginning to move the toy faster, my screams getting louder, the pinwheel rolling over my clit, screaming my head throws back, my body shaking as the orgasm takes over me, every bit of my body feeling the sensations. Gushing, I can feel something gushing out of me, panicking, I go to drop the ball. The pleasure still taking over.

"Don't panic, you're fine, you squirted, just enjoy it" His voice relaxing me, the orgasm passing, my body relaxing falling into the chair, my legs shaking, Jackson's hands removing the toys, followed by removing the nipple clamps, his hand removing the gag his lips pressing against my mouth as he slips the blindfold off. His hands gently removing the restrains, picking me up his body carrying me to the bed, lying here my body recovering from the pleasure, staying quiet, I can still feel jolts of pleasure tingling throughout my body, his hands gently caressing me.

"So, what was all that about, the only time you will do this?" My voice quiet, weak as my breathing is slowly steadying.

"Well, usually when I do things like that, I have a contract, or at least a list of what people are willing to try and not try, rules in place, but kind of hard to sit there and sort that shit out, when you're screaming during sex you need more" I can't help but smile.

"We will sort it though, then I can play without the worry that I am going to use something or do something you don't like" He is weird, so kind, yet so different in the bedroom.

"I like just about everything" Laughing at myself, I loved all that, why would I not like everything else?

"You say that now, but let's leave it for now, we can sort that another day, for now just light bondage" His lips pressing against mine.

"Let's get cleaned and eat" I love his cooking, how can I refuse? Getting out of bed, we get showered, downstairs Jackson cooks, as always, sitting down eating I can't help but smile.

"I think that was definitely the more I needed"

laughing, I can't stop the smile.

"Really? I am not too sure, even at the end, your body language was screaming for more, I know what more, but not right now" Jackson's phone lighting up, looking at the screen his whole stance changing.

"Hey Dwayne, is everything okay?" Pausing his eyes flicker towards me, his face looking guilty.

"When do we need to leave?" I don't like the sound of this, what is happening, whatever it is, he will clearly be telling me as he isn't running away to take the call.

"You know that you can always count me in, no matter what, send me all the details" Hanging up the phone his body turning towards me, I have a sense of doom, I don't like the look on his face at all.

"We have one week, then I am flying out on a mission, I can't say no, I'm sorry Alena, it is important" Wow, not expected, we spoke about him and missions and he sounded so set against it, yet he took little convincing. I do know though, I don't want him to leave and I sure as hell am not ready for him to. I have just found him, I feel like I am losing him forever again. He sat down looking at me.

"Look, tonight we are meeting for a drink, join us, you can meet the team and see that I am safe, nothing will happen while I am with them Alena" Nodding, I agree, I could do with a drink, if I have to face the fact he might be leaving I need one.

"Let's get ready" Walking upstairs, I look through the clothes I have here, not much, but still clothes, I have my own drawers and everything because my stuff keeps building up. Jackson getting in the shower, the door purposely left open, sitting on the bed watching him get washed, my body wanting him again already, not wanting, needing. Stepping out, he grabs the towel, his hand drying his hair, walking towards me, water dripping from his body, my breathing hitched, oh, I want to touch him, his towel draping across his body, covering his cock, I can't resist, moving towards him, his hand dropping the towel. Stopping in my tracks, looking up at him biting my lips, I roll my eyes, my hands stroking down his wet body.

"Shower play after" He moved, pouting my lips, I walk towards the shower, stripping I stand in the shower getting cleaned as fast as possible, watching his body dry slowly, finishing up I step out of the shower, Jackson still stood there naked and wet, walking towards him, my hands stroking his chest, his mouth kissing my lips, moaning against them, his arms wrapping around me.

"What do you want Alena?" Looking at him, my mind throws everything at me, I want the chair again, the whip, the clamps everything, and more I do know what but there is something else I want as well.

"I want you to fuck me like you hate me" His head tilts to the side, cocking a brow, his face full of humour and shock.

"I don't have time for anything like that right now kitten" My eyes roll, dropping my head I pout, sulking.

"Fuck time" His body slamming mine against the wall, the wetness of us, spreading his hands lifting me up, my legs wrapping around his body. His hand grasping my throat, holding it tight, his hips thrusting quick and hard, screaming as his cock pushes into my pussy fast, his hips moving fast instantly, his hand gripping my neck tighter, his eyes staring into mine. I barely recognise him, yet something is making me want to see more of him like this, my screams getting louder as he pushes me straight over the limit, he is giving me no mercy, the orgasm pulsing through my body, his hips pushing harder and deeper, his own pleasure rising, moaning against his body, my pleasure rising again already, his moans getting louder, my screams escaping my mouth. His hand choking me harder, my breathing free and all over, moaning I collapse against him the orgasm pushing through my body as his own pleasure rises his orgasm controlling his body and mind, his lips pressing against mine.

"You will be the death of me Alena, I swear!" His eyes looking into mine, he pulls back, his cock sliding out of me.

"I hope not Sir, necrophilia isn't my kind of thing" My eyes rolling, his cock twitching and becoming hard again, why I called him Sir, I don't know, but it had an effect on him that is for sure.

"Mmm, your cock just twitched and hardened, why was that?" I should have said, sir, it is too late now.

"Doesn't matter right now, get your arse dressed we will be late, he moved to pull me away from the wall, his hand slapping down on my ass. Getting dressed, my mind reminds me of where I am going and why, I am going to meet his team, because in a week he will go, in a week, I won't see him for I don't even know how long.

"Ready?" He looks at me, standing at the door ready to leave, I have no choice but to be ready, I am going to meet men who he sees as family, men he trusts with his life, this isn't going to be a walk in the park, my nerves are all over, what if they don't like me?

"Guess so" Walking out we get in the taxi.

"Not driving?" Looking at him, he hardly ever gets taxi's.

"No, I know the lad's so there is a chance your dragging me out and dominating me tonight" He chuckles looking at me, my face full of shock.

"Joke Alena, I don't go that far drinking, relax everything will be fine" Pulling up to a club we climb out, Jackson's arm around me walking inside the music is loud, looking around I can easily see his friends, the table looks intimidating, the men are not small, walking towards them Jackson's smile growing bigger.

"Here he is, Jacko, late as always" Someone stands

up looking at him, his eyes glancing at me, I thought Jackson was big, this guy is bigger, my eyes trailing along his body, taking in his looks, his tattoos are amazing as well.

"Hey lad's, sorry, got a little delayed, and I am never usually late, this is Alena" The guy in front of me smiles.

"Hi Alena, I am Marcus" He looks up smiling at Jackson.

"I see you found a new sub" My eyes flickering to Jacksons his head shaking.

"Not a sub, not this one, although she might be in time" I have no idea what they are talking about, but something about Marcus makes me smile. Sitting down Jackson introduces me to the other guys.

"So, Alena, can you keep this one in check, he likes wild ones" Marcus jokes Jackson glares at him, clearly thinking I will be offended.

"I can try, but then again, he is a bit rogue and well to be honest, I would rather he kept me in check" Jackson's eyes widening at my reply Marcus laughing.

"Fuck, Jackson you better watch your back with this one, she bites" Laughing at his response I shake my head.

"No Jackson does the biting, I take the bites" Marcus laughs, Jacksons hand covering his face, his hands moving lifting me, swapping our seats.

"You sit next to Troy" He looked at me smiling.

"You, talk to someone else before you turn her to be a brat like you do with a lot of subs and women you meet" Jackson's voice full of humour, yet he moved me why? Has the way we joked really offended him? Marcus moved, his head looking around Jackson's back, his hand tapping me, looking around I smile.

"Brats are the best Alena, don't let him tame you, be a brat" Jackson grabbing Marcus pulling him forward.

"Fuck sake, Marcus behave, seriously, she isn't even a Sub and you're on about being a brat" He is laughing, everyone else looking at Jackson and laughing.

"Sorry, just a bit of banter, or is it?" Marcus winks at me from across the table, Jackson shakes his head. Sitting I got to know the guys, they were nice, and I can see how close they all are as well, walking to the toilet I try to get a bit of space, too many men, all joking and laughing, and I am struggling to keep my mind clear, walking back towards the table Jackson grabs me, his body pushing me against the wall. His lips pressing down on mine, moaning I pull him to me, why do I always want him so much? His hands grasping mine, pinning them above my head, his lips pressing against my neck, my mind forgetting where we are.

"Well, this looks fun, space for another one?" Jackson's head turns looking the same way, Marcus is standing there smiling.

"Fuck off Marcus" Jackson laughs.

"Hey, worth a try, I love the redhead ones just as much as you Jackson" My face feels hot, too hot, Marcus walks off, Jacksons eyes on mine.

"Try not to wind him up too much, while you know you're joking, he sometimes forgets people have partners" His mouth kissing my neck again.

"You did good, you somehow managed to talk right back and slap him down with your wicked mouth kitten" Smiling I nod.

"Maybe I wasn't joking" Raising my eyebrows at him I smile.

"I am so going to spank your pretty little arse for that later, I hope that was a joke" His head shaking.

"It was, don't worry, I have no interest in going anywhere near Marcus, just you" Smiling at him, his lips press against mine again, his hand cupping my arse and lifting me, everything gone again, just him in my mind, moaning my hands start to unfasten his buttons, his hands pulling me up more, his mouth slowly biting down on my neck. My hands have nearly finished with his shirt, when he grabs them, his eyes looking into mine.

"No, you do realise we are surrounded by people, right? Looking around, we are, and a few people are staring, I forgot, all I could think about was him.

"Is that such a bad thing?" Joking with him, I hope he realises that because now looking around I want to hide.

"Don't push me Alena, you won't like that side of

me" His hands releasing me, that wasn't him joking, that was him being serious, now I want to know what that side of him is, because I don't want him hiding parts from me, walking back to the table we sit down. It feels weird, I am the only woman here, none of the others brought their partners it feels like I am intruding on his personal space. Marcus kept trying to talk to me, his jokes making me laugh and my comebacks just as lethal, but Jackson seems uncomfortable with the whole thing.

"I am going to go home, you enjoy your night, I will wait up for you" Kissing Jackson I try to get up, his hand stopping me.

"No, you're staying here, I want to have you by my side until I leave" His lips pressing against my neck, well that is my answer, and to be honest I don't want to walk away from him, especially with him leaving in a week.

"In that case, come dance with me" I can't help but smile at his reaction.

"Not right now, give me ten minutes, and I am all yours" Nodding, I sit back, waiting Marcus looking over winking at me.

"I will dance, come on" He looks at Jackson.

"If Jackson agrees it is okay that is" He looks at me then back at Jackson.

"Yes, just try to behave and not turn her into a brat please" Jackson laughs, nodding at him, do I even want to dance with Marcus? I can't say no, I don't exactly have a choice he is walking towards me with his arm stretched out, taking it, I stand up, his hand wrapping around me, throwing me over his shoulder, a scream escaping my lips, Marcus laughs, Jackson doesn't look to happy.

"Just giving her a ride to dance floor" He puts me back down, I can't help but laugh, dancing Marcus seems really nice, his hands a little too freely but other than that he is kind.

"So, you're not his sub?" Looking at him I shake my head.

"That is a shame, so you're not into the whole being tied up, and dominated then?" Looking at him I am not entirely sure if I should be talking to him about this, I am not sure if he should even be asking me these questions, but I don't want to seem rude either.

"I am, I can't say I did a lot of it before Jackson, but I am" He nodded, his eyes looking into mine, he is so big compared to Jackson, my mind wandering and thinking about him, his tattoos all over his body, I wonder if he has them on his chest and back? Why am I getting so caught up with Marcus and what he is like? He is Jackson's friend, I am with Jackson.

"I know, Jackson talks" I look at him, shocked, Jackson honestly already has told them about this stuff?

"Wow, don't freak, I don't mean what you do in the bedroom and stuff, I mean your ex Max" my body freezing at the sound of his name, Marcus's hand cupping my chin his smile soft and delicate.

"Don't worry, he can't hurt you while you're with Jackson, I tried to dig some info on him, but it is hard without a last name" I am not giving them his name, I am guessing Georgina refused as well.

"Well, I guess you're going to keep struggling because that name won't come out of my lips" He is laughing at me, why is that so funny?

"I think Jackson should know you're talking such filth to me" Jumping back, I look at him, my mouth open with shock, what did I say that was so bad?

"Relax Alena, it was a joke, you will soon learn that around ninety nine percent of what I say is a joke, sarcastic or just wrong" Laughing nodding my head I feel myself relax.

"I think you will find it is more like one hundred percent, I am yet to hear something true and not a joke or sarcastic come out of your mouth Marcus" Smiling at him, I can't help but feel happy and like he is kind, not just kind but different I don't quite know why though.

"Now, that is a lie Alena, I can speak the truth, are you ready for me to?" Do I want to say yes, his arm wraps around me as we dance, I have a feeling what he is going to say I won't like, but can I say no?

"I am ready, let's see if you can speak the truth" Smiling at him, I have a feeling I am going to regret this.

"You are pretty hot, and guarantee if I knew where Max was, he wouldn't be walking" Rolling my eyes, I laugh.

"Well, it's a good job I won't be giving out his name, just leave him be, no point you or Jackson getting locked up for being idiots. Anyway, what about you? No Wife?" His eyes looking deep into mine, my heart racing faster, turning I can see Jacksons eyes on us.

"I have a wife" He raises his hand.

"See, happily married, open relationship, but still happily married" That makes me feel better, he seems like a nice bloke Jackson seems to be closer to him than any of the other guys, you can just tell by how free Marcus acts and Jackson just taking it all in like he knows it's a joke.

"What about you Alena? Just Jackson or have you got a few men hidden around waiting to come out when you get bored?" Is that him asking if I am seeing Jackson and other guys, or is it him asking if I have guys waiting for me?

"I just have Jackson, if there are other guys hanging around, I don't know about them and they will be waiting a long time" He is looking at me like I am interesting, like I have just made everything he thought look wrong, do I look like someone who has several men waiting for me all at the same time?

"So just Max and Jackson, never had anyone else"? Looking at him I am not sure if he is going too far now with his questions.

"I am not like trying to, well, I don't even know why I asked, I was just curious, I would be surprised if you only had two partners that is all" He looks like he has realised he might have overstepped the mark asking me that, but he seems nice, and I know if anything, when I speak to Jackson about things like this, he will be told anyway.

"Before Jackson, there was no one since Max, not even a date, before Max, there was two other serious relationships, Max however, he pulled me I don't know how to explain it" Shaking my head I am trying to find the right words to say so it doesn't sound wrong.

"Basically, the first time we fucked, it was like me and Jackson, but not the same, he was dominant, and I liked that part of him. Slowly we built up what was used, I soon began to realise, he wasn't just dominant during sex, he was always dominant, controlling, stalking, and well abusive, but it was that being dominated that drew me in. Just like it did Jackson" Visions of the first time I slept with Max flooding my mind, was there signing there I missed, I can say the way he was is different to how Jackson is, but is there something that early on that I should have realised and picked up on?

"You're a good girl then" He laughs, his eyes looking at me like he is trying to take my mind of Max, like he can see that now I can't get the thought of him out of my mind.

"I would say so yes, although I have had more trouble since meeting Jackson than I have in a long time" Laughing I have to admit being with Jackson just cranked up the trouble meter.

"I know, you were pretty out of it, but I was the one who grabbed you and was putting pressure on your wounds after what Caroline did" Looking at him I now remember that he was, I have not even thanked him for helping Jackson find Liam or for coming and helping me after I ran to save him, getting myself in a lot of trouble.

"Thank you for that, for helping try find Liam and for helping me as well" I was out of it, and just remembered now that I heard his name.

"No need to thank, Jackson has been there for us many times, we would do it again tomorrow if needed, I think we should get back though, he looks on edge" Looking over he does, his eyes on us, I am guessing he is wondering what we have been talking about all this time. Walking back to the table Jackson smiled at us both, Marcus's hand resting on his shoulder.

"Nothing to worry about, just walking about how you don't rock her world in the bedroom" Marcus laughed, sitting down, Jackson's eyes rolling his head turning to me, cocking a brow.

"He is joking Jackson, I don't know him well and even I know he is joking" Laughing I rest my hand on his leg.

"Or am I? She could just be covering her tracks Jackson" Marcus winks at me, Jackson laughs shaking his head.

"I am sure if I didn't rock her world she would let me know, or at least she would say it during sex"

My hand rushing to cover my face, oh Christ I hope he doesn't say anything else, Marcus just laughs and went back to his drink, peeking out my fingers I look at Jackson, a smile on his face.

"Let's go home" His mouth against my ear, whispering quietly.

"If you are sure, I am happy to stay longer" I am, I like Marcus and for some reason he makes me feel calmer about Jackson going on this mission.

"No, let's go home, I want you to myself" His lips pressing against my neck, turning to face everyone he winks at me.

"Right boy's I am off, will speak to you all tomorrow" Everyone saying goodbye, Marcus giving me a bear hug that literally could have squashed me if he tried, walking out I can't help but smile.

"I like Marcus, I don't know why, but something about him is so different" Jacksons smile fell, what has happened in the last five seconds?

"Yeah, I was afraid of that" Looking at him, my mind trying to work out what he is so off about, is he really?

"Are you really thinking that I like Marcus enough to leave you? If you are that is just crazy Jackson" He honestly is, he thought I liked Marcus in that way, sure he is hot, but I can't see me with him.

"Sorry, ignore me, let's get home"

"Wait, what did Caroline mean by you are willing to give up what you need for me?" The thought has been on my mind for so long now.

"I don't get what you mean?" He looks confused, yet I sense he knows exactly what I mean.

"She said you're willing to give up what you need for me. That she can see I will be the one to give you what you need and if I do she will never win you back" Her words there in my mind, if I find out then maybe that is the way to stop him thinking about her, I know he does and I can't blame him for it.

"Can we forget about her please? She is no longer part of my life, at all honestly Alena, she would have said a lot to make you hate me" He clearly doesn't want to talk about it so nodding I agree to stop asking. Maybe she means him being a dominant? The fact he gave up that and having a submissive for her and is willing to leave it hidden for me. Was she trying to say I would be a good submissive and that I will be? His arms wrapping around me, smiling as his lips press against mine, the taxi stops, turning we get into it, sitting in silence, getting home standing here in the house, I remember the real reason I was scared, I am afraid I won't see him again. There is one thing I know, I am not ready for him to leave yet, I have just found him, and now I am officially going to lose him again, no matter what that thought is there what if he doesn't return?

<u>BOOK TWO COVER AND PREVIEW</u>
<u>BUY HERE</u>

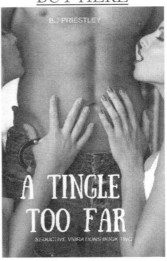

1 LIMITED TIME

Shock is overtaking me, standing here looking at him and it feel like I have limited time left in his presence. Why do I feel like this is going to be the end; Would I ever see him again? Why does he have to agree to go on this mission?

"Alena, everything will be alright" He walks over to me, his arms wrapping around my body, cradling me, trying to comfort me from my own thoughts.

"We've been on missions together for years and have never had any problems. I will be coming back to you I promise" I look up at him, how can he be so calm and so sure? It is possible he will not be coming back, no matter how small there is a chance. Embracing him I guess if he is leaving in a week I will spend this time wisely with him, I won't waste a second moping around, complaining or crying, every second I will spend with him until he leaves.

"How long will you be gone?" I smile, secretly hoping it would be a few days, but know deep down it would be longer.

"A week or two, depends how complicated things are" His eyes looking straight into mine, melting me from the inside out, two weeks, I won't say a week because there is no way I am thinking a week and him being gone for two weeks.

"Okay, so we have a week before you leave. I want to spend it with you in every possible way" I smile up at him, biting my lip, tempting him. His eyes gaze over my lip and back up to my eyes.

"Are you really already trying to seduce me?" His eyes are teasing, and his tone is making me aware it was working.

"If, I was, would you be complaining or secretly hoping I would keep going?" My question teasing as slowly my fingers trail up and down his back under his shirt. He looks at me smiling, shaking his head, I won't stop, I feel like I need to get as much of him as I can before he leaves, even if it means trying to seduce him into giving me it.

"You really are one crazy woman, aren't you? I would have thought you had enough for today, but if not…" He doesn't finish his sentence, his arms grabbing me, throwing me over his shoulder, smacking my ass and making me laugh.

"What are you doing Jackson? Put me down" I am screaming with laughter and kicking against his grip. He carries me back upstairs into the bedroom. Gently throwing me down onto the bed, his body climbing on top of mine.

"You just want to seduce me, well, it's not going to work" Jackson's head lowering as he kisses me slowly, I feel like crying that this soon will end, but I won't not until he walks out the door.

"You might regret biting your lip and trying to do that" His smile is taunting. It makes me wonder what he has planned, but to be honest, I wanted it, even though I had no idea what it was, I want everything he is willing to give me right now, no matter what it is. He is sitting there staring at me, his eyes examining me.   He looks like he was working out what to do. I can't stop the smile from growing across my face, feeling like my teasing him has thrown him, he is clearly struggling to think clearly and work out what to do with me.

"You find this funny? I am sitting here looking at you, thinking how far are you willing to go. What is enough for you and what is too much?" His eyes looking at me questioning, if only I knew that answer, I have no idea what is too much and what is enough for me. Oh, it is, he is caught off guard and is struggling to think, and I love it, smiling I bite my lip again.

"Well, we won't know until you try" I laugh at his expression, he is looking at me like I am crazy, like what I said should never be spoken in my lifetime, well I just did.

"You're pushing it aren't you? You really are crazy" His voice is filled with humour as he starts to laugh, I will miss his laugh, I will miss him.

"Okay, so we try most things? Not all right now, but

I know where to start. Last time Alena, tomorrow you are sorting out what you like and don't. I am not risking doing something you might not like" His voice is teasing yet amused like he knows what he is going to do and how I will react. I know if I beg again after he will do it, no questions asked he said he would only do it once, and this is now the second time he is agreeing without a damn list.

"I want you to strip, no questions asked, and I want you to go over there and strap your feet to that pole" I look in the direction he is pointing, it looks like the pole is on some sort of chains, like it is going to be lifted up. I feel myself panic, but at the same time excitement begins to rise inside me. I look at him with wonder as to what it is, his smile soft and delicate his only response is quick and simple.

"No questions, you have three options again, do it dressed, naked or we walk out now" I don't want to walk out, and I certainly don't want to be covered in clothing while he tries to please me. I feel brave, removing all my clothes I walk over slowly, watching him with my eyes every step I take. I begin to fasten my ankles onto the pole, finishing I stand up looking at him waiting for his next move, wondering what is going to happen next. He grabbed something leather and began walking towards me. The sight of it excites me. Pulling my arms round my back, I can feel the leather straps wrap around my arms, so they are together unable to move. He is restraining me, yet I feel so safe and calm, my breathing relaxing more. His hand slowly creeping down my stomach in-between my legs, his fingers teasing, rubbing, trying to move closer to him, but his fingers never enter, never fully pleasuring. He starts to walk around me, I feel something clip onto the restrains on my arms. He continues walking around looking at me, my heart rate slowing, my mind running away wanting more, wanting the chair again or something just as good. Is there anything better than the chair? I would have said there was nothing better than him tying me to the bed, but I was wrong, so maybe it is possible that he can do more, and the chair is just the beginning.

"Still not enough?" He is teasing me, it isn't enough, though I begin to shake my head, feeling brave, ready for anything he is willing to give me. He moves around me, his hand grabbing a flogger slowly trailing it around my body, trying to squirm as he does, my mind feeling free, just the thoughts of pleasure within it. I stand watching as he moves seductively to my side. Then, slowly his arm raising lifting it and swinging it down over my ass. I shoot up on my tip toes, smiling, waiting for more, it never feels like it's enough. He's looking at me and slowly he walks to the other side like a tiger circling its prey, while he trails the flogger along my body again. He stops at the side of me lifting it and again, swinging it down this time harder over my arse. The sting feels amazing, I can't help but jump again, my body resting on my toes, smiling, as he looks at me in amazement, I can't help it I begin to bite my lip and smile teasingly. He moves so quick grabbing me tight, forcing his kiss on my lips. He tastes perfect, I want to grab him and pull him to me, damn while I love the restraints I also hate them. It got the reaction I wanted, though, I needed him to touch me more, and biting my lip worked. He begins moving back, walking past me quickly grabbing the nipple clamps. I smile, knowing exactly what is coming as I wait excitedly. He starts walking back over to me, his head slowly lowering as his mouth starts teasing around my nipples from one side to the other. I can feel my tension grow as he teases me more and more. The flogger swinging down quick and sharp over my arse making me jump, yet I feel that isn't all he can give me, but I am not sure he will give me more or do it harder until he gets his list, his hands are seducing me, running down my side and back up again, the feel of his fingers lingering there. His hands slowly start to put the nipple clamps on me. A smile, moving across my face as I feel the tight squeeze from them. I still want more though, I want to lose all control and he can see it.

"Okay, pick a safe word. I have no idea how far you're willing to go so you need a safe word, I don't want to choose for you, so red is gone you decide not something hard to remember though" His voice is teasing as he walks around me trailing the leather flogger across my body.

"A safe word, really? Okay then how about peach?" I question, not sure why I am asking if it is okay as he told me to pick anyway. He is looking at me like he is going to laugh but he isn't.

"Okay, so peach it is. You use this word when you have reached your limit when you can't take any more. Don't throw it out, every chance you get to try and get your own way though. You say peach everything stops" His voice is right behind me and his breath rushing across the back of my neck. The fact he is saying chose a safe word makes me smile, I am getting more I know I am, at the same time though I can see in his face, he is unsure, he doesn't want to do anything that might hurt or scare me.

"If I have to gag you, which I know I will, the ball is your safe word, drop it for me to stop" He explains as he walks around the front of me. Standing here, I watch him as he wrapped the blindfold across my eyes, taking away my sense of sight, kissing me gently on the lips. I can feel my heart slowing, it feels like it is ready to just stop and fall out of my chest how is that even possible? He has not even done anything yet other than offer a safe word and blindfold me, yet I feel so relaxed. I can hear his footsteps, chains moving, and switches being turned on or off. Jumping I feel the hot liquid running down my body, slowly, starting at my collar bone running down my right side. Just as it got to my hip, the sting of the whip against my breast making my body jump slightly. I can feel him walking round the other side, hot liquid running down that side as well. Again, a sharp sting across my breast from the whip. Pushing myself up onto my toes in pleasure, wanting more moans escaping my lips. His lips teasing the back of my neck, as his hand explores my body touching every part he can reach. The flogger now running up and down me, quickly hitting my backside. I feel the sharp sting of the shock through my breasts as the clamps send vibrations through me. My moans now loud, feeling the pleasure, but still I have the feeling of wanting more, not want but need, I feel I need more I just hope he can give me it, because if he can't I know no one can. Slowly, I can feel his hands run down the back of my body towards my ankles. He stopped; slowly teasing them with his hand, while his lips being to kiss the back of my legs. I sound of the chains moving alerting me something is going to happen, I am beginning to be lifted off the floor slightly, bound to the bar, suddenly the bar between my legs spread. I am now suspended slightly, with my legs spread wide, unable to close them, gasping in shock as it happened within a few seconds. I want this, I do, and I feel completely safe with him, something I have not felt in years. His hands slowly and gently rubbing along my legs, back up to my butt where his hand swings down and spanks me hard. My body is automatically trying to push up on my toes moaning from the pleasure, but as there is no floor beneath me, I totally fail and gave in, letting him take control. His kisses starting again, from the back of my neck, teasing, and tempting as he moves in front of me. I feel I am going crazy, crazy from the pleasure, crazy from the anticipation and crazy for more of him. I don't understand though, how is he making me feel like this, like I need this in my life more than anything else. The vibrations start again from the nipple clamps stopping my thoughts, all I can think about is the pleasure, as his mouth teasing me. His lips kissing me, starting from my neck slowly moving down, until he reaches between my legs and settles there. His mouth beings kissing and teased my core, as his hand grabs my arse ensuring I cannot pull back even the slightest bit. His tongue begins to move quicker, like it is finally free to play, slowly circling the hole that longs for his touch. I can feel my pleasure rise, my moans beginning to show it, the vibrations running through my breasts and across my body. I feel the coldness of the glass running up my leg, as his tongue pushes through my gate of heaven tipping me over the edge making me scream. As the scream escapes my lips, his hand swings down and hits my ears. I muffle the sound of my pleasure, enjoying it as the glass slowly reaches between my legs and fills me, moaning out loud again and as I do his hand smacks down over my arse again. My body jumping from the sensation, moaning he can see I am still wanting more. His hand teasing me, pulling the glass in and out slowly, erratically, as his tongue gently caresses my clit. His hand starting to work faster, moving the glass at a better speed, I can feel myself growing wetter as the moisture gathers between my legs. I love it, I sharp sting of his hand across my arse making me jump, realisation hit, I was moaning so much before that spank. His body begins to move, I can feel his lips on mine, his arm stretched in front of me still holding the glass in place. His kiss is taunting and teasing. He begins moving back, and I feel the gag been placed in my mouth as his hand fastens it at the back. His mouth continuing to tease me moving down to my neck, my head moving back, giving him better access, my hands wanting to touch him, pull him to me. I would love to take control just once. Moaning my pleasure begins to build up again, his hand keeps moving faster and faster, the toy moving in and out of my pussy, making me wetter than before, my sweet essence now running down my legs. The feel of his hand placing the ball in my hands, my hand gripping it tight, I don't want to drop it and him stop. His lips starting to move back down again, teasing me as he reaches my nipple his mouth gently sucking it in. I am moaning, but there was basically no sound, the gag ensuring hardly nothing can be heard. His hand working even faster if it is even possible, he keeps going at the same speed and rhyme as his mouth reached my clit again. Jumping I squirm with pleasure, as something clamps down on my clit, the tight feeling amazing, yet painful, but a pain I seem to like and enjoy. His tongue licking around it, suddenly vibrations begin to travel through it, along my clit at the same time as the nipple clamps. My body is rocking, or it feels like it even though I know I am still. My moans are now louder, as the toy slides in and out of me at a fast pace. The pleasure of it mixing with the pleasure of the vibrations now not just on my nipples but my clit as well. I can't control it, feeling myself let I am held purely by the restraints, my body slumping as the pleasure awakens within me. Moaning my heart is racing faster, my body beginning to shake, what has he done to me? The pleasure is amazing yet at the same time it scares me. The restraints holding me in place, as I am still lifted off the ground as my orgasm grew in intensity, the vibrations and coldness mixing together making me scream. The orgasm spreading through my body, unable to move, I can feel the orgasm passing, as he slowly begins to remove the toy from me plus whatever he had previously put on my clit. I need to remember that because it felt amazing, and it is something I want him to use a lot more on me. His lips gently kissing inside my legs, not in a sexual way, but a loving, healing way. Slowly moving up to my breasts, where he removed the clamps. Once again slowly kissing each nipple before moving up and removing the gag and blindfold. Looking at him, his eyes are different, he is different this is a side of him, he is hiding a side he clearly loves, and I can see it, why does he hide something he loves and enjoys so much? Yet I can see it isn't everything, he is holding back so much. His hands releasing me from the restrains, wrapping his arms around me he begins to carry me to the bed, lying there he smiles down at me.

"You are amazing, I honestly expected you to say the safe word" His smile is teasing like he is assessing me but amazed. I cannot help but smile back, my whole body and mind relaxed and free how is that possible?

"Well, clearly you know exactly what I will like without even asking, you just know. I am surprised though that you would choose a relationship over the freedom you could have with your business"

It is the truth, it amazes me so many men would love to have his business and the freedom to use it at will, yet here he is in a relationship unable to enjoy the business fully. I don't understand it, sure when he created it, obviously he used it, but why give it all up, why not find a way to still get to use the business.

"I used to, then I met Caroline, we dated, and I don't even know how we became to date, I didn't date but with her I did. I put that part of my life behind me. I would be just as willing to do the same for you if you didn't like any of this. Caroline didn't even go to Seductive Vibrations, she refused, saying she wanted nothing to do with it. That is how against it all she was, my playrooms were set up before I met her, I gave up everything for her. So, I would easily give up all this for you" His hand motioned around the room. I now realise what he is saying. Caroline had not been into anything like this, he has had this part of his life hidden for years. I feel like he was opening up to me and telling me things I didn't know, and he was willing to tell me.

"It is not like after Caroline I went back to it, I couldn't, it just didn't feel right, so had you been like her, I would have been fine with it" It is wrong, he shouldn't give up something he loves so much for someone, there should have been a way for him to get both.

"You shouldn't give up something you love for someone, yet you still are, I can see it in your eyes after you are fighting back so much of you, when you should just be you" He shakes his head smiling, refusing to answer, I am guessing because I am right though he doesn't say I am. Lying here we talk for what seems like hours, about what he just did, everything we can think of.

ABOUT THE AUTHOR

Billiejo Priestley, born in Leeds, in 1987. Growing up, writing poetry, then slowly expanding to stories, Seductive Vibrations, a story that has been worked on for years, and finally coming available to the world.

Billiejo is a mum of five kids, showing that you can do whatever you want, and shouldn't feel bad for doing something just because society say's you shouldn't because you're a parent.

Printed in Poland
by Amazon Fulfillment
Poland Sp. z o.o., Wrocław